I0580889

SUPER HUMAN

SUPER HUMAN

Dan Pouliot

PORTALSTAR PUBLISHING, LLC

© 2023 Dan Pouliot. All rights reserved.
U.S. Copyright Certificate of Registration: TX 9-205-607

This book or any portion thereof may not be reproduced or used in any manner whatsoever without the express written permission of the publisher except for the use of brief quotations in a book review.

Printed in the United States of America

Story Guide: Masheri Chappelle
Editor: Robin Baskerville
Author photo: Gary Samson
Cover design, illustrations, & interior design: Dan Pouliot

ISBN, paperback: 978-1-7329030-7-4
ISBN, hardcover: 978-1-7329030-5-0

First Edition 2017
Self-published
Second Edition 2021
Published by PortalStar Publishing, LLC

portalstarpublishing.com
superhumanbooks.com

For allowing me all those weekends of solitude so I could get this book out of my head and onto paper, thanks to my wife, Kathy, and my son, Evan.
To my Story Guide, Masheri Chappelle: I came to you with a 44,000- word premise; and in just over a year of your masterful guidance, it became this novel.
Thank you.

For my son Evan, the original Mr. E

Part One

Discovery

ONE

Extraordinary Claims

"THE CAVE YOU fear to enter holds the treasure you seek."
—Joseph Campbell

The tap, tap, tap on the car roof announces the coming deluge. June's darkening afternoon sky makes escape that much harder. The rain hitting the roof escalates into a roar. Headlights flash on, revealing a sea of tiny dancing ripples as the driving rain strikes standing water on the road.

"Are you nuts?" WJ's mother says.

"I'm not crazy," WJ's father replies.

Screech!

"Slow down! You crossed the line again! You're going to get us all killed! Billy—Jesus!"

Screech!

The high beams of a vehicle illuminate the back of WJ's parents' heads. His mother's fingers reach to double-check his seatbelt and booster seat, feeling the buckle at his navel. The high beams from behind brighten. The harsh light forces her to squint.

"TOO BRIGHT!" WJ calls out.

"WJ, cover your eyes for Mommy! Don't uncover them until I let go of your shoe."

WJ slaps his hands over his eyes. He feels the pressure of his mother's left hand on the toe of his right sneaker. The car swerves hard to the right, pressing WJ's shoulder into the rear driver's side door.

"You're going too fast, Billy!" Mary says. "You can't see … turn off the high beams … the rain is making it worse!"

Bang! WJ's neck snaps back against the seat from the jolt of being rear-ended.

"What the hell! Oh my God, Billy! Hold on WJ!"

"I'm sorry, I brought this upon us.…"

"Look out!"

Something immense glides over the hood. A wing swipes the rain from the windshield. Billy jerks the wheel to the right. WJ's head snaps to the left.

The high beams disappear. The interior goes dark.

"What was that?" WJ's mother says.

"A bird," his father says.

"Birds don't fly in storms!"

"That one does!"

WJ's mother's eyes meet his. "Hold on WJ, we're almost home."

She twists to check him and glances out the back window.

"Billy … they're gone."

"No, they're not. I know them."

His mother studies the road behind them. "No, they're not there.

Where did they go? Oh my god, Billy, the bird is still here!"

WJ looks out his window. Even through the pelting rain, the majestic flyer is keeping pace alongside the car. A yellow eye stares at WJ, bobbing with each flap of the bird's wings.

"I'd rather a bird than them," his father says as he steals a glance at WJ and then the bird.

"Why won't they leave us alone? You told them no, didn't you?"

"It's because I told them no."

Vvvrrowm. The sound penetrates WJ's entire body; it feels like the time he stuck a screwdriver in the socket trying to fix things like Daddy. The car jostles to the right.

"What was that!" she says.

"I told you. They're still after us!"

Vvvrrowmmmmmmmmmm!

The car fishtails as it is shoved off the road. The rear passenger tire spits gravel, and a spray of rocks pelts the undercarriage.

WJ presses his hands hard against his ears and closes his eyes tight.

"It's loud Mama! Make it go away!"

"WJ, hold on!" His mother claws the air for his shoe.

VVVRROWMMMMMMMMM!

Bang!

A burst of white dust from the deployed airbags fills the car as its hood slams into a tree stump flanked by clusters of saplings at the bottom of a ditch.

The reflection of their car's headlights on the brush reveals his mother's hair draped across her airbag. Through the slackening rain, a witness stands silent outside.

Tall, head cocked, a great blue heron stares into WJ's window. It begins to peck gently at the window with its long, thin, yellow beak but suddenly stops. The heron cranes its neck to locate the source of the crunching of footsteps on gravel.

"Mary! Mary … " WJ sees his father shaking his mother by the shoulder.

The dashboard and headlights flicker. WJ's father presses the car horn and the bird takes off.

"Mary!" WJ's father says. His mother stirs. "God … help us!"

"Billy," she says. "What's happening?"

"Oh my God! Mary, you're bleeding … "

The car jostles again—then, a shattering of glass, sudden and loud, like a wave crashing against 10,000 tiny bells. WJ's mother screams and shields her face as glass shards pepper the interior.

"No! No! No! No! Mary run!"

"Billy … no!"

WJ bursts into tears.

Tattooed hands reach through the shattered windshield and grab his father. His mother swats at the hands. With one hard yank, WJ watches as the bottoms of his father's shoes disappear through the windshield opening.

"Billy! Nooo … nooo!" His mother struggles to open her car door but can't. "Billy … Billy … "

The patter of rain on the car and his mother's whimpers fill the eerie silence. She turns back to check on WJ. Her face is dazed and disheveled.

"WJ, oh my God. WJ, I'm coming," she cries. Through his tears,

he watches her struggle to open her door.

"Let me out!" She twists in her seat to kick at the door window with both feet several times but only succeeds in cracking it. His mother scrambles in her seat as she turns to reach for him. Her face, dusted with white powder from the airbag, mingles with her blood and hair, making her appear more zombie than mother. WJ screams at her grotesque appearance.

"WJ, it's okay, I'm here. We're okay," she says as she squeezes her way between the front seats to join him. "WJ, it's okay. I'm going to get us out of here. We have to get out of the car," she says frantically as her fingers fumble with the buckle on his booster seat. The straps of his seat belt slacken as she releases the buckle and pulls him into her arms. "Hold Mommy tight, close your eyes and don't let go," she orders.

WJ grabs his mother's neck and clamps his eyes shut. His body jiggles in her lap as she fumbles with the rear door handle. A gush of cool, damp air fills the car. WJ clings to his mother as she steps out of the car and into the ditch. Rain clouds, having given up their load, calm to a drizzle. WJ lifts his head from her neck and opens his eyes only to be blinded by a flood of light.

"WJ, don't look," his mother warns. "WJ … WJ … WJ …"

Bloop.

"WJ, time to wake up."

o · o · o

"Will … I said it's time to get up!" His mother's voice slips under the door. She knocks, opens the door a crack, and flicks on his lights.

Will squints hard and shields his eyes, turning off his phone's alarm. He closes his eyes.

Just one more minute ....

"WJ, now!"

Will forces himself to sit up.

One more month of school. At least I'll see Russell.

He picks up a charcoal grey T-shirt from the floor and gives it a sniff.

Acceptable.

He squeezes into his favorite skinny jeans, a gift from Auntie Joy.

"Phone, phone," he mumbles.

He lifts the shade for more light; his childhood curtains, of Spaceships and ringed planets, are gone, leaving his windows naked. Spaceships are cute for kids, but Will is past that. Underneath the window, his father's old record player sits atop the makeshift shelves-turned-entertainment-center. Its clear plastic cover, marred with soft scratches, has yellowed with age. The vintage silver turntable crowns an old Pioneer receiver. On the shelf below are records scavenged from his parent's collection.

Catching his phone peeking out from beneath the pillow, he grabs it and stuffs it in his front pocket. Will slips into his white-soled grey sneakers; they still fit well enough to make it through to summer. *Belt, belt...*

"WJ, *pick mine,*" his father's voice calls out in his head.

Will never told his mother that this happens; she might bring him to the doctor. Imagined or real, it did not matter, it was comforting.

His favorite memories of his father were walks in the woods, sitting high on his father's shoulders. Back then, he had his father to himself. His eyes catch the framed photo of him and his dad beside the turntable. It is the best photo he has of them together. He was two.

"Let's do Superman," his father would say, hands on his hips, chest out, and feet shoulder's distance apart. His steely blue eyes pretended to look off in a distance but peeked downward to catch WJ's gleeful response. Superman was done in the living room after his mother changed WJ into his footie pj's. His father got down on the rug, rolled onto his back, pulled his legs close to his body, and reached for WJ's hands. WJ held his hands out for his father to grab. He leaned his tiny torso into his father's feet, feeling their warmth through his socks.

"Ready?"

WJ giggled, grinning ear to ear.

"Here we go!" Hands holding hands, his father would lift WJ into the air on his feet.

"Okay, now let go."

WJ let go of one hand. His body wobbled, and his father's feet restored his balance.

"Now the other …."

WJ let go of his father's other hand and wobbled.

"I got you. You're not going to fall. Hold your arms out and fly."

WJ stiffened his body.

WJ let go with both hands and stretched both arms out. He saw his father's large hands beneath his outstretched arms, ready to catch him.

"Look at you … you're flying!"

WJ remembered the freedom of that moment in flight and how his father supported him.

"Let me get this! Let me get this!" His mother held the camera close and … Click. *"I got it!"*

Will studies his father's face. Even upside down, his smile showed his dimples. Will inherited just one dimple; it was a family joke that Will's right side belonged to his father, his left to his mother.

Riding his bike and swimming were his favorites. Will has become quite a swimmer; when he was in middle school, he and Russell would swim around the islands at Pawtuckaway and jump off a boulder taller than a Mac truck.

"Dad, can you hear me?" Will says softly.

He waits a moment for a response. Nothing. Will sifts through the pile of clothing at the bottom of his closet. A glint of silver catches his eye.

There it is.

He pulls out a silver-studded black leather belt. He snatched it from the attic years ago. His mother said when his father was younger, he wore it whenever he needed to feel badass. It is the kind of belt Russell would wear. Despite Russell's social challenges, he still conveyed a unique swagger.

As he tugs the belt through his pants' loops, its large studs catch on every loop. He pulls it to the tightest hole, but it is still a bit loose, causing the buckle to droop forward. A quick adjustment of the belt between the loops and it becomes a perfect fit. It feels good to fit into something.

Today, I'm the badass.

o o o

"Willis!" Russell flicks a black polished fingernail through his thick, wild black hair, pushing hair out of his eyes. His black denim jacket is bedecked with band pins, psychedelic buttons, sci-fi badges, and a UFO emblazoned across the back.

"Hey, Russell."

"Guess what I did last night?" They drop their backpacks at adjacent lockers.

"You watched UFO documentaries."

"Wait, what? How did you know?"

"I would say I'm psychic, but you wear your The-Truth-is-Out-There T-shirt whenever you go on a UFO binge."

"Yeah, I binge-watched Season Three of E.E., but that's not what I wanted to tell you."

"E.E.?"

"Extraordinary Extraterrestrials."

"You gotta cut down on UFO documentaries, people will think you're strange."

"I'm on the spectrum, people already think I'm strange. What I was *gonna* say is I started practicing leaving my body."

"*Leaving* your body?"

"You ever heard of an OBE? Out of Body Experience? I'm gonna have one. I'm this close,"—he pinches his fingers in front of his face— "I can feel it."

"How do you know if you didn't just dream you left your body?"

"A fair point— I think I'd know. What about you? Car crash dream again?"

"Yeah, but I had one before that one."

"Variety is nice. In this one, were you at least driving a car?"

"No, I'm in a field at night. I'm holding a knife and looking behind me because something's chasing me." He grabs his Physics book from his locker.

"Cool, a Bond dream. Then what happened?"

"That's the whole dream."

"Dude, that can't be the whole dream."

"That's all I can remember."

"Why, if it isn't the Freak Force. I hate to break up this nerd-fest, E.T., but you're standing in front of my locker." Rich Artman says and gives Russell a shoulder shove. "What's with all the hair gunk? It's on my jacket now." Rich brushes the shoulder of his varsity jacket, a fierce blue and gold stallion emblazoned across the back.

"Russell does rub off on you after a while. You could use a bit of his personality."

"What's that supposed to mean?" Rich presses his chest against Will's.

"Russell's my friend," Will says. "Leave him alone."

"Whatcha gonna do, Freak Two?"

"Hi Rich," Lily Powers pokes her head out from behind Will's locker door.

"Hey…" Rich smiles, "there."

"It's Lily," she says, sliding between them. "We live on the same street? We moved here last summer."

"Sure. So, what's going on?" Rich asks.

"Nothing. I just wanted to say hey." She quickly turns her back on Rich to talk to Will. Still pale from winter, Lily's fair skin and hay-colored hair suit her. She brushes a golden tendril from her eye. "Will, *My Beautiful Corpse* is opening this weekend; I was thinking of getting a couple of friends together. Would you like to come? It will be fun."

"You guys don't want to go to that yawn fest," Russell interjects. "The trailer is stupid."

"Why, Freak One, because it doesn't have aliens?" Rich slams his locker door. "I'll take you. I'll pick you up in my beemer. It's a little more comfortable than wee Willie's handlebars. Saturday night?" Rich flirtatiously taps her locker with his book.

"Actually, I have my own bike. Will, I live within biking distance from the theater, I think you do too, right?"

"Oooh, Fartman, grab a fork because you're getting served."

"Shut up, E.T.!" Rich shoves Russell hard into the locker.

"I said leave him alone," Will steps between them.

The first bell rings.

"Or what?" Rich puts his face into Will's. "I could bench

press you."

"If we get in a fight, you'll probably beat me," he says, his voice trembling, "but … you'll get kicked off the football team, which would make getting my ass kicked worth it." Will smiles and waves to the hallway surveillance camera.

"Say hi to Principal Davis! Now, what are *you* going to do?"

Pffft!

"Dude, did you just fart?" Will scrunches his face and fans the air in front of him.

"We've been gassed! "Fartman! You live up to your name," Russell says, recoiling from the stench.

"It's Artman, Freak One!" He fires back and gives Russell one final shove as he retreats down the hallway.

"Your fart was worse than your shove!" Russell hollers at Rich as he walks away.

"Stallions!" Rich whoops as he approaches a small group of his teammates, right hand in the air for high fives.

The second bell rings.

"We're late," Will grabs his Physics book.

"Will, what you just did was really cool," Lily says.

"Not really. I could have gotten my face smashed. But I had a good feeling he wouldn't. My heart is pounding out of my chest," Will slams his locker door. Turning to head to Physics, he notices Lily is smiling as she waits for him.

o o o

"My mother said the angels were beautiful, and they are really beings of infinite love and patience. The angels that came to her told her the Earth is a classroom," Allie says, combing her fingers through her chocolate brown high ponytail. She lifts it to examine it for split ends as she speaks.

"God, Allie, you're so transparent. You can stop campaigning. You're not getting any more likes. No one believes you," Ivy says under her breath.

"Ivy, your words are like your name-poisonous. Spsstttt…" Allie sprays an imaginary spray towards Ivy. "Weed, be gone!"

"Grow up, toddler."

"I believe her," April interjects. "I had an angel experience. But the one I saw didn't say anything. I just saw it when I got caught in a riptide and almost drowned."

"Really…" Allie says.

"It's true. It's like Allie's mother says. There is that light." Ivy rolls her eyes.

"Ivy, I don't care what you think. I saw it."

"Come on April, really?"

"Yes, and I will never forget it.

"What flavor Kool-Aid did you have with your breakfast this morning? Grow up, people. Live in the real world." Ivy grabs her books and moves to the front of the class. Lily, Will, and Russell slip in the door just before Mr. Bohr closes it.

"I'm so glad you three could make it," Mr. Bohr says.

Lily makes her way to Ivy's abandoned seat.

"Hey, Lily!"

"Hey, Allie," Lily sits and quickly unpacks her backpack.

"Hey, Russell," Allie says, biting her lip.

"Hey, Al,"

"It's Al*lie.*"

"I know, but I like Al better."

"Al is a boy's name."

"Not necessarily. Al is short for Albert, Alan, and Alexander, which is the male version of Alexandria. In today's world and understanding of one's sexual orientation, Al has become gender-neutral.

"Whatever," Allie says, turning her back on him. "As I was saying, my mom says many of these angels that walk among us don't even know who they really are—they think they're regular people. Nobody told them they're an angel, so they're completely oblivious! They have to figure out on their own that they're angels. They asked my mom, 'How would you live your life differently if you learned you were an angel?' Ever since then, she's been a completely different person; she even apologized to people she hurt in the past, including me."

"So," Allie finishes, "which one of *us* is the angel?"

"Thank you, Allie. Every time I hear your mother's story it inspires me," Mr. Bohr, hovering close by, interjects with coffee-scented breath. "But this is a science class. It's time to close your mouths, open your books and your minds. As Carl Sagan said, 'Extraordinary claims require extraordinary evidence.'"

Mr. Bohr's unruly and disheveled, once-red hair, along with his bulbous nose atop his prodigious mustache, might mark the brilliance of a genius too caught up in matters of the universe to bother with such petty considerations as *grooming.* His oversized glasses and potbelly round out a persona so cliché it might as well be a costume.

"So true, Mr. Bohr," Russell says. "But, check this out … I can bend a spoon, with my *mind!* Who's got a metal spoon? Anyone?" He points out across the classroom. "Anyone? No one? Oh, wait …" Russell reaches into his pocket. "I happen to have one *right here.*" With a flourish, he pulls a metal spoon out of his pants pocket. "An everyday, normal spoon," he tells his audience. "Here, inspect it for yourselves," he passes it around.

Allie scrutinizes it. "Is this spoon clean?" She holds the spoon with two fingers at arm's length, her nose wrinkled. "Perfectly harmless. A bit of dried yogurt from yesterday most likely." His face turns to glee at her attention, and she passes the spoon back to him. "Now that you have seen that this is just an ordinary spoon from an ordinary kitchen, watch closely, as the *extraordinary* is about to take place right before your eyes." With rapt attention, excepting for Rich, the class watches as he grips the spoon tightly in his right hand, holding his arm out straight in front of him so all can see. He closes his eyes. "I'll quiet my mind, so I can gather energy from the universe. It works better if everyone watching does the same." He pauses for a long moment, peeking briefly to gauge the audience, breathing slowly and deeply. He opens his eyes. "This metal's warming up, I can feel it softening." He brings his other hand up to grip the spoon, then, with a rapid flick of his wrists, the spoon bends, not a bit, but around itself three times.

Audible gasps come from the class.

"You look like you've never seen magic before," Russell says to the class, grinning ear-to-ear.

"How did you *do* that?" Mr. Bohr asks.

"You're the Physics teacher, you tell me! A little metallurgy and physics … and psychology; people gladly fall for a lie that lets them escape their pathetic realities. It's not hard. Tutorial available for $14.99 from AmazingWoodini.com. Or I can teach you … for the low, low price of $29.99." Russell tosses the twisted spoon to Mr. Bohr, slides back into his seat, whips back his hair like a heavy-metal lead singer, and then pulls a handful over his right eye, Criss Angel style.

"A quick round of applause for our resident magician," Mr. Bohr says, locates his glasses, stowed in the V of his v-neck sweater vest, and perches them at the tip of his nose. He inspects the spoon and unsuccessfully attempts to twist it. "Let's return to business … where's my spotlight?" he chuckles. "Who can recap what we learned yesterday about atoms?" He points to the only student to raise a hand. "Lily?"

"… That subatomic particles are so far apart that they are mostly made of space?" She turns to Allie when she hears a textbook drop to the floor.

Allie scrunches her nose and mouths: *brown noser.*

"Correct, Lily. We're surrounded by mostly empty space; even physical objects like this table,"—he gives it a rap—

"which feels utterly solid. Physical objects have vastly more open space in them than particles." Mr. Bohr adds, "If we removed all the space between all the atoms in the Earth, our entire planet and everything on it would take up the space of a football stadium."

Will writes in his notes:

Mostly space. What's in all that emptiness? Extra dimensions?

"Time for a new lab," Mr. Bohr announces. "Find a partner and pair up. Come up, get your lab books, and go find a table."

"Hey Al, want to be my partner?" Russell asks.

"In your dreams."

"Dreams are good. I can make that happen."

"I'll be your partner," Ivy tells Russell.

"Will, want to be my partner?" Lily asks.

"Uhh … uh, sure," Will says, ears burning.

o o o

"Is everyone clear on their lab assignment? Follow the guidelines on your instruction sheet and we should see some pretty interesting results." Mr. Bohr says, checking the time. "Report is due Tuesday, and I want conclusions to show a clear chain of causality. You've got a few more minutes of class, I recommend you use it to set up your working schedules."

"That's a good question," Lily says.

"What is?"

She reads from his notebook, "'What's in all that emptiness? Extra dimensions?' Totally profound. Mr. Bohr's mind would be blown if we made that part of our hypothesis."

Will chuckles.

"So, shall we meet at your house or mine?"

"Why?"

"We have to discuss the theory and come up with our hypothesis before we do the labs. It's due Tuesday, which isn't a lot of time. So, we have to meet after school to work on it."

"Yeah ... right." Lily's piercing eyes made him feel naked. He kept his eyes on his sheet of paper to avoid looking at the gentle swell of her breasts, which was peeking out at the point of her v-neck. He pops his head up to find her blue eyes staring back into his. He turns away and fiddles with his textbook.

"How are we going get this lab report done on time?"

Don't look at her breasts. Don't look at her breasts ...

"Well," Will says, "I guess we'll need to work on it together."

Duh— idiot!

"We don't share a study hall."

"Should we work on it, um ..."

Don't look at her ....

"At your house?"

"I was gonna say online."

"Oh." She shuffles the papers in front of her.

Idiot, idiot, idiot!

"But I suppose… you could come over."

"Okay, but I don't want to wait until the last minute."

"Yeah, I guess we should get a jump start." Will rubs the back of his neck.

"Yeah, I want to stay on top of this lab."

He could not stop himself; his eyes found her breasts again.

"Yeah, we should definitely keep abreast …."

Pervert!

The first bell rings.

"I mean… you wanna come over to my house after school today?"

"Sure!" She glides her hair back behind an ear and lets out a big, satisfied exhale. She slides her things into her backpack, failing to contain her smile.

"I'll meet you at the front entrance. We can bike to your house."

"K…"

"It's a date. See you at 2:30." Lily spins on her heels. Her cheeks are lifted by the smile on her face as she leaves the room.

"My bruh has a date at 2:30," Russell raises his hand to high-five Will.

"Put your hand down, it's not a date. We're going to get together at my house to work on our hypothesis for our lab."

"Do you have to meet her at a specific time?"

"Yeah …"

"At a specific place?"

"Yeah …"

"You have an activity you are going to do together?"

"Yeah …"

"That's a date. I know you like her, and she likes you. Take my advice and enjoy the fact that Lily is crushing on you."

"Can't."

"Why not?"

"I got gym next … with Fartman."

The second bell rings.

"Freeman and Laforce, you're going to be late for your next class."

"Willis, just be thankful it's not dodgeball."

Russell stops under the classroom door. "What gives, Mr. Bohr?" Russell points at the dim LED light above the jamb. "Your cool detector must be broken because my spoon trick was sick. Does that light even do anything?"

"You're the magician," Mr. Bohr quips, "you tell me."

Mr. Bohr raises an eyebrow when the light blips as Will exits.

TWO

Dinner at The Freeman's

"Can I help with the dishes, Mrs. Freeman?" Lily asks.

"Nonsense," Mary says. "You're our guest. Will can clear the table."

Lily gets up and grabs her plate, careful not to disturb the chess game at the end of the table.

"No, Lily, please sit. Last I checked, WJ still has two hands. Let him clear your place."

Lily offers Will her plate and mouths, "Sorry." He brings it to the sink, his ears growing warm.

He flicks the switch for the over-the-sink light. Clickety-click. The fluorescent light sputters, making a little noise but no light. Will flicks the switch off and back on. He flicks it several times. "Can we replace this light? The plastic's turned all yellow. It doesn't even turn on half the time. It's junk!"

His mother comes over and places her hand on the switch. "Think kind thoughts to the light," she tells Will. "Thank it for turning on, then flick the switch." She pauses and closes her eyes. She flicks the switch; with an audible clickety-clickety-click, the light flickers and stays on.

"Oh, come on," Will says. "You got lucky. I warmed it up for you."

"Now, where were we?" She returns to the table.

"You don't believe that New Age crap, do you?"

"I do believe 'that New Age crap,' and you'd be wise to broaden your thinking."

"Mr. Bohr says, 'extraordinary claims require extraordinary evidence.'"

"Mr. Bohr," Mary gives Lily a playful tap on her arm. "Don't you love it when people's personalities match their names? FYI, WJ, the evidence I've experienced is extraordinary enough for me."

"Like the time you thought you saw an angel?" He makes air quotes behind her back.

She turns to Will, "I'm not crazy. I saw her, and you did too; you just don't remember. She saved both of us."

"Mom, *you* saved us. You were probably in shock and running on adrenaline."

"No, she saved us."

"Mrs. Freeman," Lily says, "that's the third angel story I've heard today."

"Disdain is not a flattering look for you WJ. You want evidence? Try this: Ask a question before going to bed. Ask anything. See what happens. Lily, Thomas Edison would nap sitting in a chair with a steel ball in each hand and a metal tin on the floor under each."

"Oh?"

"He did this so when he was on the verge of sleep, he'd wake himself up to capture his subconscious thoughts. Thomas-Flipping-Edison, you guys."

Bwoop. Lily checks her phone. "Mom's texting. That's my cue."

"Well, Lily, it was a joy having another woman in the house. Do you need a ride?"

"Thanks, Mrs. Freeman," Lily says. "No, I've got my bike. It's only a few miles. Bye, Will!"

"Bye."

His mother waits for the door to click shut. "Bye? Is that the best you can do? I have a lot to teach you about women."

o o o

His room illuminated by the glow from his phone, Will cracks the window to let in the sound of peepers. He pulls back his blanket, slips between the sheets, and fluffs his pillow. As his phone blinks off, Will wonders what question he should ask.

Not that it matters, this won't work.

He wakes up the phone and checks the alarm. off.

"What will I be when I grow up?"

No, that'll take too long.

"Tell me about tomorrow?" He puts the phone back on the nightstand and pulls up his covers.

Too vague. I know plenty about tomorrow. Tomorrow's Saturday. It will still be spring. The forecast is sunny. I'll have breakfast, lunch, and dinner; and likely hang around the house all day.

"Can you tell me something about tomorrow I don't know?" Satisfied and proud of his question, he closes his eyes and relaxes into his pillow. His phone's display goes dark once again. He dozes off as a few slivers of moonlight sneak past his pulled shades.

o o o

Blackness. Void.

What is this?

"Is he ready for what's coming?"

Who's that?

"He's smart."

"Doesn't matter. He's stubborn. He's unaware."

"Lead Council, most adults are unaware."

"Yes, unfortunately, that is true. The boy is almost sixteen, and he does have a keen sensitivity that is undeniable. Additionally, I think he possesses more wisdom than most of the adults we tried to help. If given the time and our support, I believe his mindfulness will blossom, and his abilities will grow."

"Lead Council, I am grateful you see what I see and recognize his potential."

Who's talking?

"Yes, we all see what's in his heart."

"Lead Council, I contend his fears control him. He abdicates his *responsibility. He lacks faith; he refuses to consider any perspective that challenges his own."*

"And I contend he's capable and willing."

"He's indecisive."

"Indecisive? Really? How is that any different from what we are doing, challenging our positions to arrive at a consensus?"

"He lacks courage. Let's not forget the others. They failed miserably."

"They didn't fail. They weren't ready. There's a difference."

"They were unable to open their eyes."

"I feel he has the capacity."

"It's not whether he has the capacity; failure could crush him. He's not ready for Infinity."

A hint of light reveals seven men and women in timeless linen tunics standing together next to a pond.

"Council, who among us has ever been ready for what's next? Fail miserably. Fail again. Until one day, you fail a little less. The next day less; and the next. That's what growth looks like. Struggle mightily even when it feels like it's too much to bear."

Lead Council turns. "What are you doing here?"

"Who, me?"

"See? He's already demonstrating his powers. That's more than capacity."

Oh, crap.

"Relax, Will."

Will's eyes pop open. He checks his phone to see what time it is.

11:11

What was that? Was it a dream? Did I leave my body? Where did I go? Who were they? I have to tell Russell.

"Relax."

Will drifts back to sleep.

THREE

The Change Purse

"WJ, let's explore!" Will's father calls to him to enter a shallow cove underneath a rocky outcropping at the edge of the beach. Sunlight bounces off tide pools; their reflections dance on the dark walls.

Along with various colorful fish, a raspberry octopus swims past him in midair. The octopus stops, lifts a tentacle, and Will lifts a hand. When the two touch—like a passing shadow—the octopus' pigmentation shifts from crimson to peach. It pushes off Will's hand and floats towards the back of the cove, where Will finds Lily in a raspberry-colored top. She is radiant, her hair billowing.

Will steps with care as he moves from sand to seaweed to rock. The sloshing of water in these shadowy tide pools echoes off the walls with a rhythmic bloop, galump, bwoop.

The octopus reaches out a tentacle and pulls Will closer to Lily.

She raises both hands, holding something out to him, light pouring from her cupped hands like a water fountain. Bloop, galump, bwoop.

Bwoop.

His dream vanishes at the sound of his phone. Forearm over his eyes, Will turns his head to the nightstand, hoping the texter will go away. *It's Saturday morning. Ugh.* He unlocks his phone.

His phone rings. He waits a moment before picking up, but the caller hangs up. As he stares at the *Missed call* from Lily on his phone, it rings again, and he picks it right up.

"Hey, Will! Whatcha up to today?"

"No plans," he attempts to sound awake. "Why?"

"I thought we could work on our lab."

"But it's Saturday."

"Okay, then let's do something else. I don't have plans either," Lily says. "So … why don't we have no plans together?"

"Sure, uh … yeah, okay, that sounds good."

"Now?"

"Um, right now?"

"Yeah, right now. No, silly, I have to bike over first."

"Ah, haha. Yeah, right. Sure, now works," Will says, jumping out of bed and scrambling for clothes.

"See you in a few!"

o   o   o

"Psychedelic," Lily turns the album over. "Klaatu?"

"Yeah, people thought they were secretly the Beatles."

"Cool. Can we listen?"

"It's a little weird."

"I like weird." She takes the album out of its sleeve and opens the turntable's lid. Will turns on the receiver. "Is this how you do it?" Lily places the record on the platter. "Where's the on button for the record player?"

"It turns on when you move the arm over the record."

Lily and Will both grab for the arm at the same time, fingers nearly colliding. They both pull back and grab for it again, halting short of touching. They both chuckle.

"You do it," Lily says.

"No, you do it," Will says.

"Yay," she grins and lifts the arm. She moves it over the platter, and it starts to spin.

"The orange light tells you when the record's spinning at the right speed," Will tells her.

"Move the needle right here," he says, pointing to the outer ridge of the record.

The pleasing pops and crackles that come out of Will's

speakers make her smile.

"The turntable was my dad's. Mom helped me restore it a long time ago. It needed a new needle, belt, and oil. I had a lot of fun with it … I don't use it as much anymore."

The song starts with sounds of trudging through a marsh at dusk, giving way to dulcet vocals accompanied by flute and synth. The vocals begin tenderly. As Lily closes her eyes and listens, Will studies her grin.

"A song about telepathically contacting aliens? Cool …" Lily picks up the small, framed photo from next to the turntable. "Is this your dad?"

"Yeah."

"How old were you here?" She offers him the picture.

"Three." He returns it to the shelf.

"I can see the resemblance."

"Will," his mother says, with a courtesy knock. "Oh, I thought I heard voices. You two slipped right by me."

"Hi, Mrs. Freeman!"

"Hi, Lily. Will, I wanted to warn you your Uncle Rod is coming over. I made the mistake of mentioning the light over the sink, and he insisted on fixing it," she rolls her eyes. "Anyway, I'll leave you two to it. I mean … I'll …" She shakes her head and mutters, "never mind." His mother closes the door, then opens it … just a bit.

Lily snickers. "She left us to it!" she smiles. Will blushes. "You got any other trippy albums like this one?"

"Hmm. Not much here, but my parent's … my Mom's

record collection is up in the attic."

"Ooh, can we go see if there's more?"

"Sure."

"It's a little creepy up there," Will says, leading her to a door in the upstairs hallway.

"Creepy? That means it will be better than *My Beautiful Corpse,*" Lily says with a smile.

Will opens the hallway door to reveal bare wooden stairs going up and around a corner, wrapping around the chimney. The attic floor is makeshift, planks laid down—not even nailed in—across insulation and joists. The single, bare light bulb and tiny window at the end are not enough to light the space.

"Creepy never bothers me. Creepy places have the best treasure."

"Here," Will points to a few milk crates filled with old albums. "My mom says the most loved albums are also the most worn."

"Awww," she sits cross-legged on the dusty, unfinished pine boards.

"Monty Python records? Nerd alert! Ooh, The Graduate. There's a gem. I love Paul Simon," Lily shows him the cover as he joins her on the floor: a young man's gaze is transfixed on a woman's leg in sheer black pantyhose.

"Here's one," he pulls out a black and white album of a lady in a white suit wearing opaque white sunglasses. "Laurie Anderson."

"Artsy," she says. He sets it down beside them.

"What's in here?" She pulls back the flaps of a half-closed cardboard box.

"Some old junk."

"Pants, pants, pants," she says, rummaging through the contents of the box. "Are these your dad's?"

"Yeah, my mom is a hoarder. Long story. I'll tell you later." Spying books and more underneath, she pushes aside the folded pants with the enthusiasm of a treasure hunter.

"*Journeys Out of the Body*—is this your mom's?"

"Probably Dad's."

From the assorted knickknacks, Lily picks up an item about the size of a plum. It's light and hollow. It resembles a miniature football if footballs had three sides. She turns it over in her hand; each side has a symbol on it:

"Does that long story include this?" Lily holds out the tiny football. The vision of his morning dream flashes in his mind.

Even her top is the same.

He takes the item from her. "Mom!" he hollers and bolts
downstairs with Lily on his heels.

"What's this?" He hands Mom the tiny football.

The smile leaves her face. "Where did you find that?"

"In one of the boxes in the attic."

"Hm. That belonged to your father … it's a change purse,"
she says, handing it back with forced nonchalance.

"Isn't it strange for Dad to have a change purse? It's not very
manly," he says, jamming it into his pants pocket.

Lily giggles awkwardly and blushes at the oddly shaped bulge
protruding from his skinny jeans. His mother takes one look
at Will and turns her head to stop from laughing. Turning his
gaze downward, Will blushes when his eyes catch the bulge.

"Oh!" He spins around, "Haha." he jams his hand in and
yanks out the change purse, his inverted white pocket
dangling limp against his jeans. He stuffs his pocket back into
his pants.

"Your father was into some strange things. Sorry, I didn't
mean it that way. Your dad was a terrific person, and the
things he was into were all good, great even—*strange*—but
great." She gazes up and shakes her head. "Okay," she mutters
and holds out her hand, "Give it to me. I'll show you." Will
hands over the change purse. She holds it between her thumb
and forefinger and pinches. Her pinch squeezes the internal
tension rods, and it opens along one of its seams. She glances
in and releases her grip, closing the purse.

"I think it's neat," Lily says. Mary hands it to her, and Lily tries pinching it open and closed a few times. "Look," she says, "there are papers inside!" She holds it open for them to see.

"Your dad would want you to have that. It's yours if you want," Mary says, peering through the kitchen window. A shiny, black Dodge Charger pulls into the driveway past the kitchen window. Its engine releases a low growl that increases when the driver revs before removing the key from its ignition.

"Woah! Whose muscle car is that?" Will asks.

"Oh, God. It's your Uncle Rod. I forgot he said he was coming to fix the light. Is that a new car?"

"Great, just what he needs … a muscle car." Will grimaces.

"WJ, he can't help it. He's your father's brother. Be nice."

"That's the problem. We're always nice to him."

His mother opens the knickknacks drawer. "Put that away …."

Will chucks the change purse into the drawer.

Uncle Rod steps out of his vehicle, pats his hair in the side view mirror, inspects the car's finish, and flicks an invisible spot of dust off the hood.

"What a douche," Will mutters.

"WJ, language."

"It's true."

"I know … but he's still your father's brother."

"What's he doing now?"

Rod dodges the spray from their floral-shaped lawn ornament. He follows the hose back to the house and turns it off. Water beads glisten and drip off the nearby lilacs. Will's mother said lilacs were his father's favorite. After his father disappeared, they moved to this house. His mother planted two lilac bushes and said she was looking forward to the day his father would be able to smell them with her. Will never understood what she meant by that, but he enjoyed the thought of his mother and father sharing a love for something.

Uncle Rod swaggers up the steps to their kitchen door, pulling at his khaki camouflage pants.

"Hi, Rod. Thanks for coming over," Mary says, opening the door for him.

"Oh, hi, Mary … no problem. I'm glad to help. I turned off your sprinkler to save on your water bill. Like the new car?"

"Oh, is that new?"

"Yeah, I was thinking about going green and all, but you know, a man's gotta have his power." He winks at Will. He turns back to Mary. "Anything new to report?"

"Stop asking me that. I'll let you know."

"Hi, Will. And you are?" Rod holds out a hand for Lily.

"This is Lily," Will says.

Rod shakes her hand and winks at Will. "Sweet … you found a sport."

"Rod, the light's right over here."

Rod flicks the switch a couple of times. "Ballast. Pretty

common issue. You should go LED. You'd save on your electric bills. Every penny helps when you're on a fixed income. I replaced all the bulbs in my house. I can replace this for you if you want. Fixture's about $30 … I wouldn't charge you for the labor, of course."

"Well, that's generous of you."

"Hey Will, like the new khakis?"

"Those aren't your old ones?"

"These are the real deal; Desert Storm approved … got 'em at the surplus. Just because they wouldn't let me in doesn't mean I can't be ready to serve at a moment's notice. You wanna come to the hardware store with me? I'll teach you how to replace a fixture."

"Thanks, Uncle Rod, but … "

"Learn about taking care of your home; it keeps you grounded. You don't want to end up like your father."

"Rod!"

"What? He knows I'm kidding. Don't you, Will? As for you, little lady," Rod says, wagging a finger at her, "treat my nephew right, and he'll never have a reason to …" his voice trails off.

"I really appreciate you stopping by," Mary says, opening the door. "The kids have a hectic schedule this afternoon and I need to make them lunch …."

"Lunch? That'd be great. Keto?"

"Keto?"

"Ketogenic."

"Yes, I know what it's short for. I've heard *of* it. I just don't know what it is."

"Low carb, high fat, all the basics … eggs, tuna, extra virgin olive oil, almonds, avocados, butter—preferably grass-fed if you have it, but if not, I understand. Body's a temple, right, Will? Nothing sugary, no grains, no root vegetables. You should give it a try, Mary, it'll help with your, ah … *metabolism.* Maybe like a chicken salad with olive oil and feta? It'd be good for Will's brain function too."

"I'll keep that in mind. Low carb, high fat," Mary says through clenched teeth.

"Tell you what, I'll head over to the hardware store before we eat and pick up a fixture for you. My treat."

"That's generous of you, Rod, but I want to pay you." She grabs the doorknob to let him out, and his hand lands on hers. He smiles and gives her hand a quick, gentle squeeze. She withdraws her hand; he opens the door.

"Hey, Will? I'm opening up the cabin this weekend. How 'bout you and me head up? Seclusion, off the grid, just you, me, and some fresh air. It'd be good for you to have a father fig—"

"Gee, that's quite an offer," Mary says. "Will and I will have to talk about that."

"Yeah, let's definitely talk about it," Will says.

Mary closes the door and locks it.

"I'll be back in time for lunch!" Rod calls out from the other side of the door.

"Don't make me go back to his cabin *again*," Will says. "I went three times, and every time was torture. I'd rather have my teeth drilled."

"Of course you're not going. I was being polite. He can be difficult, but he's been going through a rough patch since Joy left him. Show him a little compassion."

"I bet Dad wouldn't," Will says, irritated.

"Your father knew the value of compassion. I wish I could get that through to you. Your Uncle Rod may be too far gone, but you still have options." She opens the drawer and tosses him the change purse. "Explore your options. Lily, would you like to stay for lunch? Tuna fish sandwiches and fruit salad. Keto!"

"Yes, thank you."

"You two can hang out in the living room while I make the fruit salad."

"Come on," he says to Lily, and she follows him.

Will has a seat on the couch and turns the change purse over in his hands.

Lily plops down in the adjacent pleather recliner, draping a knee over the chair arm closest to Will, and bobs her foot in his direction. "Sooo … WJ? Will Junior?"

"She calls me that when she's trying to embarrass me."

"Well, I like it." She corrects her posture and leans forward. "Can I see?"

"Sure," Will perks up and hands her the change purse. She peeks inside again, "Let's check out these scraps of paper."

She gets up from the recliner and joins him on the couch. She removes the papers and spreads them out on the coffee table in front of them.

"'I ask for answers, and I get them,'" she reads, her voice low, serious, and an eyebrow arched. She grabs another. "'I treat people with kindness.' Aww, that's sweet. 'I don't let my fears get the best of me.'" She turns to Will, "This is like some bizarro fortune cookie." She chuckles at her own joke. Her glee leaves her face when she reads the last one to herself.

"'WJ is safe from harm.' This fortune cookie went from cute to creepy."

"Let me see." Will grabs the scrap of paper.

"I've never seen this," Will says. "That's not creepy, that's crazy." He tosses it onto the coffee table.

She slides the papers aside, opens the purse wide, and holds it up for closer inspection. "Hey, there's some words on the inside in the fabric on the back." Stitched in golden thread on the red silk lining, she reads: "'Activated Consciousness.'" She wrinkles her nose. "What the heck do you think *that* means?"

Will stares at the coffee table.

"Hello? Earth to Will. Does any of this make sense to you?"

She asks, "Where's your dad?"

"He left when I was young."

"Oh?"

"You sound surprised."

"When your mom talked about your dad, it sounded like she still loves him."

Will turns on the couch, placing a leg on the cushion, and turns his torso to her. "He left after the car accident. For all I know, he's dead."

"Oh my God." Lily holds a hand to her mouth.

"He's not really dead, but … we don't know. It was a long time ago."

"What happened?"

"My mom doesn't like to talk about it, but it was raining, and we got into an accident because he was driving too fast. That's what I remember. But my mom says evil men forced the car off the road and abducted Dad, and that an angel saved us. Uncle Rod thinks he went nuts and left us. Everybody has their version of what happened."

Lily places her hand on Will's. "I'm sorry, I had no idea."

"Anyway, it was after that we moved to this house, and we've been here ever since."

Mary pokes her head in. "Lunch is almost ready. I'm missing a cantaloupe for the fruit salad and chips for the sandwiches. I need you to run to the store," she extends a ten-dollar bill.

"What about Uncle Rod?"

"Don't worry, he's getting a bagged lunch. Hannaford's is not even a mile. Take your bikes, and you'll be back before him. Remember to press the bottom of the melon like I showed you and smell … "

"Mom!"

"Go!"

FOUR

Put That Thing Away

"Don't forget to smell it," Lily says as she fiddles with the change purse.

"These are cold … smelling them doesn't work. You gotta press the stem in, like this, to see if it gives."

"Uh-huh," Lily pinches open the change purse. "Oops." It bounces off the cantaloupe display and onto the floor. The two knock heads as they both crouch down to pick it up.

"Oh, I'm sorry!" Will says, rubbing his forehead.

"Bonk!" Lily says with a chuckle. They both grab for the change purse. Lily grabs it first. Will's hand lands on hers. Lily smiles, and Will yanks his hand away.

"You should be a little more careful with that."

Will turns to find a man standing in a pair of red and black Air Jordans. Above them are well-worn jeans and an unbuttoned plaid shirt over a "CALM DOWN, you're scaring the children" T-shirt. A Native American man is looking at him and pulling at the pocket of his shirt. He removes a nearly identical change purse.

"He has one, too," Lily says.

"You don't know what you have." The man pulls out his wallet, finds a business card, and offers it to Will. "Why don't you come by? I'll tell you about it if you want to know."

"Keep your card."

"Relax, Will," the man says.

Will jerks his head back in shock. Lily takes the card.

"You can call me Joe." He adjusts his Red Sox baseball cap, sitting atop a cascade of black and grey hair pulled back in a loose ponytail.

Lily reads the card aloud:

Rise and Shine with Master Wen

Consciousness Coach

Awareness

Mental Fitness

You Are the Drive.

"You are the drive?" Will says. "What the heck does that even mean?"

"Shush," Lily says. She flips it over and reads the address:

1111 Eleventh St.

Rockfield, New Hampshire.

"Hey, Eleventh Street is the shortcut I take to get to your house." She hands Will the card.

"How did you know my name? … where did he go?" The two look around, but there's no sign of Joe. Will grabs the closest cantaloupe. "Let's get out of here."

○ ○ ○

"'Consciousness Coach,' what's up with that?" Will says to Lily as they step out of the store.

"Well, the change purse says, 'Activated Consciousness' on the inside. Maybe they're related. This is the first time either of us has ever seen that thing, and we happen to run into someone who has another one just like it." Lily says matter of factly. "That's not a coincidence."

"Sure it is. I bet he's a serial killer or something."

"A serial killer with another change purse? He knew your name. And why would he tell you to relax?"

"I don't have a good feeling about this."

"I'm spooked too, but aren't you the least bit curious?"

"Kinda …"

"So what if it's not a coincidence? Is that going to stop you?"

"Stop me from what?"

"Finding out why he has the same change purse."

"I don't know …."

"We can ask him. We don't even have to go inside the house," she offers in her most reassuring voice.

"We're not going to his house."

"Will, it's just a conversation."

He stuffs the cantaloupe into his backpack and zips it. He gets up and presses his hands to his pockets. "I have an idea. I don't have my phone on me. Can I see yours?"

"You're calling him?"

"No, I wanna do a search."

She unlocks her phone and hands it over.

"Activated consciousness," Will says and taps the first link. Their two heads come together as Will scrolls through the site.

"Weird. Looks like some old, classified government document."

"It's too hard to read. How come it's so blurry?"

"It's old." Will swipes down and finds a fuzzy, black-and-white photo.

"What the heck is that?"

The grainy, over-copied photo is of a windowless room. But it's the large object on the floor of the room that leaves them speechless.

"That's nuts."

"It's the same shape as the change purse!"

"Yeah. But a lot bigger."

"A.C. Shell. In neutral state," Will reads.

"A.C.? Do you think that stands for Activated Consciousness?" Lily asks. "Swipe up."

"That's the end of the page," Will says.

"No, wait, what does that say? The sun is making it hard to read."

Will changes the angle of the phone. Like a slow dance, they shift their bodies until the glare of the sun on the phone is gone.

"'To learn about A.C. drives, click here.'" Will reads.

"Click on the link," Lily urges. Will taps the link, and the screen goes haywire. "Uh oh, virus, virus!" Like a hot potato, he drops the phone onto his backpack.

Lily grabs her phone. "What do I do? What do I do?" She tosses it to him.

"Quit the browser. Close it!" He tosses it back.

Lily presses the Home button. "Nothing's working! Nothing's working!" She tosses it back.

Will presses Home repeatedly, but nothing happens. He closes his eyes and takes a deep breath. "Please work!" He presses again. This time the button works, and the screen returns to normal. Will breathes a sigh of relief.

∘ ∘ ∘

"I don't feel like watching TV tonight," Will says. He scrapes the last bits of dinner off his plate into the trash and drops the plate into the lower rack of the dishwasher. "The last dish is in the dishwasher. Can we finish our game?"

"I don't know if I'm ready to concede," his mother replies with a smile as she bites into a cookie and closes the pantry door with her elbow. "You've already captured half of my pieces. Have you no pity on an old woman?"

"No, and you're not an old woman."

"You're sweet."

"You can thank me after I capture your king and put you out of your misery," Will says, taking his seat at the end of the dining table. "I will show you mercy. I will try to make this round short and painless."

"Whose turn is it? I don't remember where we left off."

"Yours. I'm about to capture your queen."

"Oh, right. Now I remember." She starts the timer on her phone and studies the board. She keeps a finger on her queen as she inspects a possible move. "I like Lily …."

"We ran into this strange guy at the store who had a change purse just like Dad's."

"What strange guy?"

"He gave us his card," Will reaches into his pocket and slides the card across the table to her.

"You're trying to trick me into taking my finger off my queen. I have two hands," she quips and grabs the card with her free hand. "Master Wen?"

"He told us his name was Joe," Will adds.

"Joe? Was he Native American?"

"Yeah, why?"

"Crap," she mutters, lifting her hand off her piece.

"Now your queen belongs to me."

"No, that's not my move." She moves her queen back.

"You took your hand off the piece; we're doing takebacks now?"

"Time out." She stops the timer. "Did Joe say anything to you?"

"He said I should visit him if I want to learn about the change purse."

"No. You're too young." She nearly disrupts the chessboard getting up from the table and goes to the kitchen.

Will follows her and stands in the kitchen doorway. She grabs the sponge and begins to wipe down the countertop, the stovetop, and the refrigerator. "He's too young," she mutters. She looks him directly in the eye. "You're not ready."

"Not ready for what?"

"That purse … there's a lot that you don't know. Once you found it, I knew it was only a matter of time. I didn't realize it would be this soon. Dammit!" She throws the sponge into the sink, grabs a dishtowel to dry her hands, and heads back to the dining room. "It's your turn," she announces, pointing to the chessboard.

"Mom, what's going on?"

She stares at the chessboard. "Were you thinking of taking him up on his offer?"

"What do you think I should do?"

"Don't let what I think to be part of your decision. Forget about me. What do you want to do?"

"You seem pretty stressed out. I think I should skip it."

"What did I say? Don't let my feelings make your decisions," she says, fighting back tears.

"I was thinking maybe I can find out something about Dad."

"Your father …"

"I wasn't going to say anything because I knew you'd get upset. But you always told me that I could tell you anything." Using a clean corner of the dish towel, she wipes the tears from her face and grimaces. "This needs to go in the hamper," she tosses the dish towel for Will to catch.

"Does this mean you're throwing in the towel?" Will asks with a nervous smile.

"This is the wrong time to have your father's sense of humor."

"I got one dimple and his sense of humor; at least he left me something."

His mother snorts a chuckle, takes a deep breath, and exhales. "You're not a kid anymore. Somehow you grew up, and I missed it."

"I wouldn't say that. I still need you to do my laundry. I won't go if you don't want me to."

"No, you can go. I trust you."

"I'm not going to join anything. I just want to ask about the change purse."

"Joe and your father go way back. You can trust him."

"If you would just tell me what really happened to Dad, I wouldn't have to go."

"I've told you again and again, but you never believe me. Your father was taken. Now you can ask Joe." She twists her hair into a quick knot. "It's my turn to make a move."

Will watches as she slides her last pawn up to his queen.

"You're throwing away your move. Are you giving up?"

"Try me and find out."

FIVE

Master Wen

"This is the address," Will says, double-checking the business card against the number on the mailbox. The house sits in a tightly-packed yet well-to-do neighborhood. The two-and-a-half-story, buttery yellow Queen Anne Victorian is adorned with cerulean and burgundy trim.

"The good news is it doesn't look like a serial killer's house, right?" Lily asks.

"How do you know what a serial killer's house looks like?"

"Would a serial killer have one of those on his front lawn?" She points to the wrought iron wind wheel, covered in a patina of rust: a dappling of orange, red, and brown. A gentle breeze starts half of the curved blades moving. After a moment, the remaining blades begin turning in the opposite direction.

"Hey Will, that reminds me of your sprinkler. Oh! Did you see that?"

"What?"

"When the blades line up, they form the shape of a flower!"

"I feel like I'm in an episode of *Charmed*," Will remarks, dropping his shoulders with a sigh.

"I love that show. You watch *Charmed*?"

"My mom does. She's seen the whole series a dozen times."

"Your mom is so cool."

"Yeah, she is."

"Let's go in before you change your mind," Lily says, grabbing Will by the arm and leading him up the walkway to the front door. A sky-blue door jamb frames a red wooden door; the door's vertical inset panels have been painted sky blue and lime green, while the horizontal center panel is yellow. Each panel sports orange trim, making the door bright and cheery.

"Are we really doing this?"

"Yes. Besides, there's nothing but good witches in here. And look at their doorbell. It's adorable. It's like an old-fashioned, windup toy. It even has instructions on this brass plate. Look, it says, *'Turn.'* It's the kind of antique my dad would have." Lily is about to twist the doorbell handle but stops. "Give me your hand." She grabs his hand.

She's holding my hand!

He studies her solitary silver ring. The band is narrow with a light-blue stone. It matches her eyes. Her short fingernails are painted a soft pink; the nail polish is chipped in all the right places. No girl has ever touched his hand.

"You ring the doorbell," she says, placing his hand on the handle.

Following the instruction, he gives the handle a twist.

Brrringgg!

After a moment, the door opens. "Welcome, we've been expecting you." A black woman greets them. Her patterned skirt and white top complement her skin. "Please, come this way," she says, offering them a soft smile and leading them from the Zen-inspired foyer into the central parlor.

"This is so beautiful," Lily mumbles as her head tilts back to admire the high ceilings and ornate woodwork. "You have a beautiful home. How old is it?"

"It was built in 1881. Would you like some tea?"

"Yes, we would love some tea," Lily says eagerly.

"Oh, okay," Will adds.

"I'll be right back. You two make yourselves comfortable."

"Will, can you believe this place? This house is amazing. My dad would kill to have this. Not literally, obviously, but he would love this house," Lily says. "Holy moly!" Lily exclaims as she disappears into the next room. "Will, you've got to see this!"

Will enters the space. His eyes are locked on Lily as she spins in a circle, her mouth agape.

The spacious central parlor opens wide in the back to a sunny addition: the conservatory is light and airy; the three exterior walls are glass, framed by a warm cherrywood trim. The vaulted ceiling is capped by a large skylight.

"Will, do you see this? Is this real?" Lily asks. Will's eyes follow her finger that points to an artfully manicured Japanese black pine that reaches to the skylight. Above, a handful of sparrows chatter in the tree's branches. "They have a tree inside their house!"

"Is a tree larger than a person still called a bonsai?" Will asks.

"How come you're so calm? They have a tree inside their house!"

"I can climb that."

"It's not for climbing; it's for admiring. I want one of these in my house!" She steps over the threshold from tile to dirt and passes a hand over the bark of the tree. It resembles parched earth.

"What's the point of growing a tree in your house if you can't climb it?"

"The tree even has an ant. Hello, little guy," she says.

"Do you think that woman was his wife?" Will whispers.

"She had no ring. Did you see her necklace?"

"No."

"The leaf with the letters a, i, e on it? But the letters were all together like Celtic—like this," she pulls off her ponytail holder. The black elastic ponytail holder is adorned with a pewter disc about the size of a silver dollar. The disc is decorated with a braided, rope-like pattern.

Heading back into the parlor, Lily points to the bottom half of the wall. "I think that's called wainscoting, popular in old houses."

"Hello there!" Joe walks in to greet them with a big smile and arms outstretched.

Will bows awkwardly and extends his hand for a handshake. "Hello, Master ..."

"Ha, we haven't *mastered* anything." Joe grabs Will's hand with both of his and gives it a vigorous shake.

"I'm Will, and this is Lily."

"Nice to meet you, Joe," Lily says, holding out her hand.

"Nice to meet you, Lily! Old business cards ... we don't say 'Master' anymore."

"That tree's spectacular!" Lily says.

"Isn't it? The world's largest air freshener," Joe jokes.

"How old is it? And how did it get in here?" Lily says, rubbing its bark.

"This part of the house used to be the greenhouse. The owner back then kept it in here, and the tree did so well that when it got too big for its pot, he planted it in the dirt floor. We love it too."

"You've even got birds in here," Lily says.

"They come and go when I open the skylight. Come, let's sit," Joe motions them towards a table and chairs close by.

"Your business doesn't have a sign out front," Will says.

"We don't advertise. Our students find us."

"Students?" Will asks. "This is a school?"

"Short answer: yes."

"Look, if you're trying to enroll me in your private school, I don't have any money. The only reason I'm here is to find out what this thing is," Will says, placing the change purse in front of them.

"Yes, yes, no worries. We'll get to that. But to really understand what that is, it takes a while to explain. And about the whole school thing, don't worry about that either. We don't want any money from you. The only expense you will incur is your time … and your effort."

Effort? Will raises an eyebrow.

The woman returns and sets a tray with a teapot and three cups on the table.

"Will, Lily, this is Mira. Mira, Will, and Lily are the ones from the grocery store."

"Pleased to meet you. I made jasmine tea."

"Are these cups antiques?" Lily asks. "My dad was into antiques."

Will grabs a cup. "Check out this one. Are the cracks filled with gold?"

"Kintsugi," Mira says. "It means 'golden seams' in Japanese. A broken cup can never be unbroken. Instead of hiding the evidence of its fall, we mend it with care. That way, the memory of the trauma is honored."

"That's real gold filling those cracks?"

"Yes, that's real gold."

Lily inhales deeply over the tray and lets out a slow, happy breath. "The tea smells amazing … like flowers. I *love* it."

Mira pours them tea. "Be careful it's very hot."

"I feel like royalty." Lily pretends she's at a high tea party, extending her pinky from her cup.

"Mira," Joe says, "we have a potential problem, here's another one. Sorry about that." As he lifts his spoon out of his tea, the spoon droops like a wilted flower.

"You've got to be kidding," Will says.

"Kidding?"

"You're messing with me. Spoons don't do that."

"Oh? What are spoons supposed to do?"

"It's a trick spoon," Will grabs the spoon out of Joe's hand. Will's expression changes, "This is metal …."

Mira brings a box of spoons from the kitchen and a vase of fresh-cut flowers.

"We buy in bulk." Joe grabs a fresh spoon.

Will hands Lily the spoon for her to inspect.

"You can do this, too," Joe adds.

"For $19.99? I'm not interested in magic tricks," Will says.

"No, a box of spoons costs $9.99 at Walmart."

"You think that was a magic trick?" Mira asks.

"Was it?"

"You regard your inner wisdom as an affront to your intelligence," she sets the vase on the table. She arranges the flowers, moving a white rosebud on a tall stem to the center of the arrangement. The bud slowly opens in front of them.

"Whoa!" Lily exclaims.

"How did you do that?" Will asks.

"That's a sign for us all," Joe says, "that we're all meant to be right here, right now."

"How gullible do you think I am?"

"Gullible? I think you've bought into consensus reality," Joe says.

"Consensus reality?" Lily asks.

"Ever heard of St. Joseph of Cupertino?"

"My mom's religious, but I'm not," Will says.

"Lily, how about you? Heard of him?"

"No."

"Joseph was an Italian priest in the Middle Ages. He had a habit of spontaneously levitating. He lived during the time of The Inquisition—bad for him but good for us—the church kept meticulous records. There are over seventy separate accounts of him levitating. Sworn testimonies of witnesses who saw him do it. To say he levitated would be an understatement … he flew.

"What do you think the church did about him? They didn't want anything to do with him because he was a distraction. So they shuttled him from monastery to monastery, often in the middle of the night, but where ever they tried to hide him, crowds kept finding him and wanting to hear from him instead of the priests, so the Inquisition placed him in isolated seclusion. His only crime was he couldn't stop levitating. It took a hundred years after his death for them to make him a saint."

"Wow," Lily says.

"Wow is right. He multiplied food. He healed people … I could go on, but he's not the only one. Why haven't we heard of them? Because it doesn't make sense. It doesn't fit. That's consensus reality."

"I dreamt once I floated above my bed," Will says.

"Could be a dream. Or could be something else."

"I was asleep. It must have been a dream."

"Small thinking keeps you small. You know the truth; you just let your doubts run the show. Relax your mind."

"Why does everyone keep telling me to relax?"

"It's not as easy to have an epiphany when you're clenched." Joe grabs a new spoon, blows on his tea and stirs, and takes a sip. "That's better."

"We have to go." Will stands and gives Lily a hard look.

"Why?" Lily asks.

"We just have to go."

"I'm so sorry," Lily says.

"I understand." Joe gets up to escort them out. "We didn't go over the change purse today, but we will next time."

"We can come back?" Lily asks, trying not to lose Will as he bolts out the door and descends the steps.

"When you come next is up to you. Will, you're welcome to come, too!"

Lily descends the stairs. She turns around to wave at Joe as he closes the door. "I'm so sorry."

Lily catches up with Will. "Dude, you were rude. O. M. G. That was amazing!" She says, climbing on her bike. "Did you …"

"Wait until we're down the street," he says under his breath.

Will hops on his bike and pedals to the intersection. Lily follows him around the corner, but he shows no signs of slowing down.

"Wait up!" Lily calls out, trying to catch up to him. "Will, stop!"

Will stops, plants both feet on the ground, and waits for her. Lily screams as she jumps off her bike, dropping it to the ground. "What is wrong with you! That. Was. AMAZING!"

"That guy is a psycho."

"That's because you doubted it."

"Look, this isn't a movie. This is real life. He's not Yoda. I can't explain what I saw, but Russell or some other magician probably can."

"I get it. They're strangers. But I *like* him … her too."

"I'm not going back."

"Will, you're being cautious—and that's a good thing—but I think they really want to help you. If anything, go back to find out about your father."

He lifts his handlebars and bounces his front tire on the pavement a couple of times."Ugghhhh." He squints an eye at her sideways. "Okay … fine."

"Tomorrow, same time?" Lily asks.

"Tomorrow, same time."

"Pinky swear." She holds out her pinky.

"How come you bite your pinky nail?" he asks.

She hides her hand behind her back. "Everyone gets one bad habit, right? My father used to put bitter apple on it so I would stop."

"I like it." He extends his pinky.

"You're weird." She extends her arm and pinky once again.

"Say it."

"Say what?"

"Pinky swear. Otherwise, it doesn't count."

"Oh right. Pinky swear."

"Great. I'm holding you to that."

She hops on her seat and pushes off. "See you tomorrow!" she calls over her shoulder as she peddles away.

She likes me!

He punches both fists in the air.

After she's out of sight, he turns his bike around to take the shortcut home. Seeing Joe heading to the mailbox, Will slows to a stop a safe distance away. After grabbing the mail, Joe spots Will.

"Did you forget something?"

"I rode with her to the end of the street … but my house is, well … it's just easier for me to go this way."

"Some shortcuts can be time savers. Others … you lose yourself in a maze of side streets and alleys." He snaps the mailbox shut.

∘ ∘ ∘

"How did it go?" Will's mother asks.

"He's a spoon bender," Will replies, watching her folding laundry on the couch. "Big whoop."

"Spoon bending. Yeah, that sounds like Joe." She places his

folded pants on a free spot on the couch.

"How come you never told me about him?"

"We decided it was best to let you discover things on your own when you were ready."

"Who's *we?*"

"Joe was in your father's group."

"Group?"

"Your dad had a group he used to go to a couple of times a month. I talked with Joe a lot. Cheerful guy … he had a great laugh. He showed me a bent spoon once; he was into that sort of thing."

"So is Russell. It's all just magic."

"You think there's no such thing as real magic? Everything's connected. You, me, that light in the kitchen, everything. And that's not for nothing. That's for something. And that car accident? Your dad didn't cause it. We were *pushed off the road.*"

"By another car?"

"No. There was another car, but no, it wasn't like that."

"Then what?"

"I'm not ready to talk about that."

"Why not?"

"Because … because I can't explain it. All I can tell you is it happened. I felt it. I was there."

"Extraordinary claims …"

"WJ, stop it. My experiences are real. Don't gaslight me."

"Gaslight? What does that mean?"

"When you try to make someone think they're crazy because you don't like what they have to say." She snaps a towel open. "When something doesn't fit their models, righteousness isn't scientific. It's stubbornness and a bad case of pride."

Will scrunches his face.

"I recognize that look," she says as she squares away piles of clothing. "I remember what it was like being a teenager. I thought I knew everything, too. Boy, was I in for an awakening. Here's your laundry," she taps a neatly folded pile. "Let's finish our game." She twists her hair into a knot and moves to the dining room.

Will follows her in. "Good, you gave me your last pawn; let's get this over with."

She picks up her queen and puts it down next to his king.

"Ha. You could've blocked me with your knight." Will goes to grab her queen.

"Wait," she says. "Look at the board."

"What?"

"You can't take my queen with your king because that would put you in check from my rook. And if you move your king, you'll be in check by my bishop. You have no more moves. My pawn was just bait, and you took it. Checkmate."

Will studies the board. "You won? You've never beaten me."

"I let you win. The bad guys won't let you win. Ever. Joe's your teacher now."

SIX

A Terrible Liar

"Time is a measurement of energy or force in motion. A measurement of change. By that definition, Russell, you're late."

"Sorry, Mr. Bohr. I don't mean to interrupt. Continue with class. Oh, wait, about the finals—are there gonna be any questions about wave-particle duality?"

"I can neither confirm nor deny the existence of that question until I see it." Mr. Bohr's quip is met with blank stares. "That was a wave-particle duality joke. Wave-particle duality was a fun detour—for me. Since you brought it up, and since there *may* be an extra credit question on the final, here's a lightning refresher on the topic," he says, erasing the chalkboard.

"To appreciate how mysterious wave-particle duality is, we need to start with classical mechanics. Classical mechanics is also called Newtonian mechanics because of whom?" He cups his hand to his ear.

Russell answers, "Isaac Newton."

"Correct. And what legend is associated with him?"

Russell answers again. "He was sitting under an apple tree. An apple fell and hit him on the head, and that's when he got the idea for gravity."

"Right, again. The laws of gravity: A body at rest will remain at rest. A body in motion will remain in motion unless it is acted upon by an external force, etcetera, etcetera."

Will writes:

classical mech = gravity, body at rest, force, motion

"Classical mechanics describes how the macroscopic world works." Mr. Bohr tosses his chalk in the air and catches it. "But the subatomic world operates by a different set of rules. Max Planck noted particles don't always behave like particles. Sometimes they behave like waves." He draws a cloud, like a scraggly ball of yarn, on the chalkboard. "Quantum mechanics says particles also behave like waves, a cloud of possible locations where the particle could be, like a field of potential."

Max P. particles = waves = field of potential

Will's fingers slacken around his pen; his eyelids grow heavy as Mr. Bohr drones on. He lowers his head to conceal his closed eyes. "Field of potential" echoes in Will's mind as he drifts off.

"If you want to measure something, you need to observe it, right? Measuring subatomic particles necessarily involves interacting with them … bouncing a photon off them, for instance. When we interact with them to take a measurement, we call that *observation*.

"Guess what happens to that cloud of possibility when we observe it? It collapses down to a discrete particle." He taps his chalk hard on the chalkboard. "That's called the collapse of the wave function, and it happens when we make an observation. Quite possibly the biggest mystery in physics is *when you observe the subatomic world, your observation changes it.*

"Sometimes a wave, sometimes a particle: wave-particle duality. Does this ring any bells? Will? Wake up."

Will opens his eyes and sees Mr. Bohr standing over him.

"Oh, uh. Sorry." Will shakes his head to bring his attention back to the room. "No, I was thinking about what you said."

"Would you like a pillow?"

Will's classmates chuckle.

"Actually, I was thinking about what you said."

"Oh? You could hear me while you were sleeping?"

"I was listening."

"Tell you what. Since you were such a good listener while you were asleep, I'll add wave-particle duality questions to your final exam for extra credit." The class does a collective groan.

"You all can thank Will for that extra credit."

The bell rings.

"A final reminder everyone, your lab reports are due tomorrow."

◦ ◦ ◦

Will and Lily prop their bikes up against the blossoming cherry tree in Joe's front yard. Will loops his chain around his bike and spins the combination lock. Lily locks up her bike too.

"Come on!" Lily says, bounding up the stairs, and the front door opens.

"I'm glad you two decided to come back!" Joe says, leading them into the conservatory.

Will starts. "I only came back because I have questions. Once I get answers, I'm out of here. Why didn't you tell me you knew my mom? She says you knew her and my dad. It wasn't a coincidence we met in the grocery store, was it?"

"Coincidence? Depends on your perspective. Yes, I knew your parents." Joe walks past the tree and sits on a wicker couch. He pulls his change purse out of his pocket and turns to Will. "I don't bring this with me much anymore, but I had a feeling I was going to need it. When I saw yours, I knew why." He hands his purse to Lily to examine.

"Your purse is more burgundy," she says, turning it over. She quickly peeks inside, then closes it.

"These belonged to a group of us. We found each other through … I'll call them *synchronicities*. We learned we had similar, strange experiences—spontaneous downloads we couldn't explain."

"Downloads?" Lily asks, "like on your computer?"

"No," Joe says. "Or maybe. Yes, to my computer … this one." He taps his temple.

"Where's the group now?" Lily asks.

"We disbanded when we found out we were being hunted."

"Hunted?" Will asks. "Why?"

"For our ideas. Some people thought the information we had gotten … received … was too dangerous. We didn't know who we could trust; we were afraid to involve the authorities. So we split up. We don't maintain contact; that would only make it easier for them to track us down."

"Who was hunting you?" Lily asks.

"The A.U.," Joe says.

Lily furrows her brow. "A.U.? That's the symbol for gold."

"Agents of Unchange," Joe explains. "Your father was one of us," he tells Will.

Will's face contorts. "What happened to my father? Is he dead?"

"Like your father, you have special abilities; you just don't know how to use them yet."

"You didn't answer my question. Is he dead?"

"No, he's not."

"He's not dead? Do you know where he is?"

"Your father is lost to us … he's not retrievable. Ever since he left, we've kept an eye on you. I have. And now you're here. Are you ready to pick up where your father left off?"

Walk out the door.

"I … we need to go. We have a test tomorrow."

"We do?"

"We need to go study. Come on Lily." Will spins on his heels and walks into the trunk of the tree.

Thonk!

The sparrows chatter at the disturbance.

"Will, are you okay?" Lily asks as Will brushes off his shirt.

"That's gonna leave a mark," Joe quips, "not on the tree." He spins his baseball cap around and points to a mark on his forehead. "We're brothers now."

"I'm fine, I'm fine," he says, barely looking back and making a beeline to the front door.

Lily rushes to keep up with Will. She looks back at Joe, "Sorry … Will, wait up? Will heads down the steps double-time. "Will … "

"What!"

"Why are you angry at me?"

"I'm not. I'm angry at my father," he replies, unlocking his bike.

"Will, you don't know what happened. You didn't give Joe a chance to tell you."

"It doesn't matter. I know enough. My dad's not dead."

"But that's good, isn't it?"

"He's lost to us? He's not retrievable? What does any of that mean? And the A.U.? They hunted my dad? And if that wasn't weird enough, I have special abilities? Pick up where my father left off? This is nuts!" He yells, shaking his bike as he tries to free it from its locking cable.

Relax.

"And stop telling me to relax!"

"What? Who's telling you to relax?"

"Nobody … forget it!"

"Wait. Will, what's going on?"

"Can we just forget it? I wasn't talking to you. This is the weirdest day of my life. This is crazy!" He unlocks his bike lock and yanks the cable.

"Crazy? This is more sane than Mr. Bohr's physics explanations. This is real life," she says, unlocking her bike. They walk their bikes off the lawn.

"I'm supposed to believe my dad was hunted?"

"Doesn't that make him one of the good guys? Think of it this way: all this weird stuff is worth it if you find out why he left."

Will studies Lily's face. Her encouraging smile lifts four soft freckles sprayed across her nose.

"Sorry." He repeatedly squeezes the bike' brakes.

"Will, I get it. My father left us too. I would kill to find out why my father just disappeared from my life," she wipes a wayward tear from her cheek. "If I had a chance to find out why my father left us behind, I would take it." Lily's blue eyes swell with tears. Will wants to kiss her like Mike kisses Eleven in *Stranger Things*, but their bikes are in the way. Instead, he settles for tapping his handlebar against hers. "That's what I like about you."

"What?"

"You're always right … and you know it. You're confident." They stand in silence on the curb, straddling their bikes, their handlebars touching.

"Will, we'll get answers. But you need more practice getting yourself out of awkward conversations."

"I thought I was believable."

"No, you're a terrible liar … but I like that because it means it's not in your nature," Lily lifts up onto her seat, steps down on the peddle, and pushes her bike forward.

"You're going?"

"Are you coming?" she calls back, glancing over her shoulder. He sees her smile through the blinding sun as she turns the corner. He jumps on his seat and peddles as fast as he can to catch her.

SEVEN

Ta-Da!

Allie raises her voice to carry over the din of the busy cafeteria. "Lily, Lily! I saved a seat for you!" Allie taps the blue stool next to her.

Lily approaches, tray in hand. "Why would you save a seat for a brown noser?"

"I didn't mean it like that. You're just so damn smart, it makes the rest of us look bad."

Lily takes a seat. "New T-shirt?"

Allie runs a hand over the front of her sparkly, "I'm no angel," T-shirt. "Hey, you haven't followed me on the gram yet."

Lily tightens her lips. "I'm not on *the gram*."

"We have to rectify that. Your nails … yikes. Use the gel polish. It won't chip. See," Allie holds up her shaped and painted nails.

"Are those press-ons?"

"No. These are my real nails," Allie says pulling back her

hands.

"Sorry."

"I forgive you. So, what's up with you and Will? I saw you leave school Friday *and* yesterday with him."

"We had to finish the lab report."

"Uh-huh. I'm in Physics, too. Olivia and I didn't have to leave school together *twice in a row* to finish it."

"You two have study hall."

"Come on."

"We went to Will's house to work on the lab report."

"See? How hard was that?" Allie takes a long bite of her sandwich. "I heard Rich likes you."

"I don't care about Rich. He's a jerk."

"That's because you have a thing for Will. Hmm … *Will* she or won't she?"

"What does that mean?"

"The beast with two backs, girl! *Sex!*"

"Ugh, it's not like that. Is that all you care about, sex? There's more to life than hooking up with some guy so he can brag about it to his jock friends."

"You do know Will's dad went bat-shit crazy, right?"

"What?"

"That's why they had to move."

"Who told you that?"

"My dad is hunting buddies with his uncle Rod. You better hope it doesn't run in the family."

"Will is not crazy … he's shy … and a little stubborn."

"Will is in his own little world; he thinks he's better than everyone else."

"You don't know him."

"Rich is more sophisticated, not moody. Sure, he's a bit conceited, but I'd rather deal with too much confidence than not enough. That Russell's kinda cute, in a weirdo sort of way. Not for me, of course, but maybe for someone more his type."

"His type?"

"You know … weird."

"Weird?"

"I didn't mean it like that. He's just a bit … unusual sometimes—all that alien talk and his geeky jacket. He needs a makeover. It makes sense that he and Will are good friends. With Will, you never know what you're gonna get. If that's what you want, so be it. As your bestie …"

"Bestie?"

"I got your back … if you ever need an alibi."

"Alibi? For what?"

"You know, time between the sheets …"

"Eeewww, I told you it's not like that. Will is not a horny dog." She grabs her tray and leaves the table.

"Don't blame me if you have little psycho kids!" Allie hollers.

o o o

"Ta-da!" Russell whispers as he removes a slice of cold pizza in plastic wrap from a brown paper bag.

"I had the strangest dream last week," Will says. "It didn't feel like a dream. I was in darkness. I knew I wasn't awake, and I knew I wasn't asleep. I can't describe it."

"Pure awareness … that's some serious yogi stuff right there. Do you have any idea how long grown-ups take to attain that? There's something about teenagers and our sponge brains."

"Hold up, it gets weirder. A group of people was talking about me."

"Sounds like you met your council."

"Huh?"

"Your council. We all have one. They watch over us, keep us on track."

"Why would we have a council watching over us?"

"Why wouldn't we?"

"There aren't any higher beings hovering over us. We're it."

"How would you know?"

"All this talk is making me crazy." Will shoves a forkful of mac and cheese in his mouth.

"I have that effect." Russell chomps into his pizza.

"I had that running-in-a-field dream again last night."

"Again?"

"Pretty much the same as before. I'm running away from this thing I can't see. Someone else is running with me. She tells me to put down the knife so we can go faster."

"She? Who's she?"

"That's not the point …"

"Is it Lily?"

"I'm trying to tell a story."

"It's Lily. No sweat dude, s'all good. So you dream about

Lily. Totally understood, she's cool. Wait a minute … that's why you sat right there, so you can watch Lily!"

"Can we not talk about this?"

"What's the big deal? You like Lily, no big whoop. Okay, okay … fine, you were telling me about this dream."

"That's the whole thing."

"You're running in a field at night with a knife, and Lily tells you to put it down."

"Yeah, but it felt like I was going to die. I wanted to wake up."

"You can."

"Huh?"

"Yeah, you can … with practice. Throughout the day—whenever it occurs to you—think, 'this is a dream.' Make it a habit, and eventually, you'll be right. Or maybe this *is* a dream."

"Don't look now, but Lily's coming this way," Will says. "I said …"

"Hey, Lily!" Russell says. "We were just talking about you."

"Mind if I join you?" Lily asks.

"We'd love to have you, isn't that right, Will?"

Will laughs awkwardly.

"Will was just telling me …"

" … We were talking about his spoon trick."

"Oh, spoon bending," she says, having a seat. "Russell, you're into magic. Is that all a trick?"

"You mean, do I think all spoon bending is magic?"

"Yeah."

"Learning magic is great because you learn all the ways to deceive people. But when you're watching a magician, you're in on it. You're a willing participant in the deception. If you aren't fooled, you're disappointed. In a way, magic is the most honest profession. When other people lie to you, how can you tell? Magic keeps me looking for all the ways someone might be lying to me.

"But that doesn't answer your question: do I think spoon bending is a real thing? If you believe I bent that spoon with my mind, you're gullible. If you dismiss it all as merely magic, you're cynical. I've never seen legit psychokinesis. But I keep an open mind … skeptical, but open."

"Don't look, here comes trouble," Lily says.

"Three's company, but four's a party! I thought I'd bring the party to you." Allie takes a seat next to Russell and grabs his hand. "Is that a gel?"

"No. Gel nail polish can damage the nail. Picking at your gel manicure like you do is bad for your nails. You're not just peeling away the polish but the top layer of your nail, too. This damages it, weakening the nails, so they are more prone to rough textures and white patches like the ones on your right ring finger. It also makes them more susceptible to cracking and breaking. You might want to stop using the gel polish and go back to a regular lacquer that has a mix of an organic polymer like what I'm wearing: it's called onyx, like the crystal. Criss Angel has onyx nails. Onyx, they say, grounds you and clears away confusion. It brings focus and confidence in your ability to make good decisions. I carry one in my pocket and put the energy of the crystal on my nails. Wait, those are press-ons, right?"

"God, you're a freak! Can't you have a normal conversation?" Allie grabs her tray and leaves.

Russell fidgets with his paper bag, then suddenly balls it up and tosses it across the table in anger. He pounds his fist on the table, causing Lily to jump before he goes quiet.

The bell rings.

"Russell, don't listen to her … Russell? Will, is he okay?"

"He's upset."

"I thought he said he doesn't care what people think of him."

"He doesn't … until he does."

As the cafeteria empties, Lily and Will remain with Russell.

"Will, what do we do?"

"Nothing. He'll come back."

"Come back?"

"Sometimes when he gets upset, he retreats into his shell."

"Can I stay?"

"You'll be late for your class."

"It's just study hall. Retreating into a shell … some days I could use that."

Will puts an arm around Russell. "He likes the weight… like a weighted blanket."

"It's being a good friend," Lily says. "Should I hold his hand?"

"I don't know."

"Hey Russell," Will hugs him, "Allie's a jerk." Lily rubs Russell's back.

The second bell rings.

"For the record," Lily says, "I think Allie likes Russell in her Allie-ish kind of way, and maybe Russell likes her, too."

"Russell doesn't like her."

"Why did he go on about nail polish if he wasn't trying to impress her?"

"That nail polish lecture was just Russell being Russell."

"Really? I was pretty sure he was making a move for her."

"Please, the only one interested in Allie is Allie."

The third bell rings. The cafeteria is empty.

"Does he know we're here?"

"I don't know."

"Will …" Lily gives a nod at Russell's right hand as it moves towards Lily's and grabs it. "He knows."

EIGHT

Don't Tell the Children

"You looked upset when you left Allie at lunch," Will says, pedaling alongside Lily as they exit the busy school parking lot onto the street.

"Oh, you saw that?"

"Yeah, what was that about?"

"Allie's obnoxious. She said if I ever need an alibi, to let her know."

"Alibi? What does she think we're doing?"

"She is so superficial: her mind is always in the gutter. She thought I should be hanging out with Rich instead."

Will's tires wobble as he stands to pedal harder up the incline.

"Instead?"

"Instead of you."

Will sits down, shifts up, and coasts downhill with a smile. Arriving in front of Joe's house, they walk their bikes across the lawn to the cherry tree. When Lily reaches for her bike lock, Will says, "I got it," and wraps his chain around both bikes.

"Oh, okay— thank you," Lily smiles and once again bounds up the stairs. Joe opens the door before she can ring the bell.

"Hello, Lily. Hello, Will," he says and steps aside so the two can filter in.

"How was the test?"

"The test is next week," Lily says. "Isn't that right, WJ?"

Will gives her a long side look.

"I think he did have a test. And it seems he passed with flying colors," Joe says with a slight smile.

"Here we go again …"

"Hey, that's new," Lily says, walking over to a life-size bronze statue of a Great Blue Heron just inside the conservatory.

"Mira likes to rearrange things. Great Herons are an elegant example of self-determination and self-reliance. Those long, spindly legs don't stop them from standing on their own two feet. And such fun to watch them soar. Make yourselves at home. Mira will bring us some snacks and we can all relax."

"A big, bronze bird … beautiful," Will says. "Joe, I'm not here to relax, I'm here for answers."

Joe nods. "Telling someone to relax never works, does it?"

Will pulls out his change purse. "What do the symbols mean?"

A clatter high up in the conservatory grabs their attention; the sparrows silence their chatter.

"What's up there?" Lily asks.

"Harry is paying us a visit," Joe says.

"Oh yeah! I see it," Lily says. "Harry?"

"Harry the Heron."

"You're kidding …" Will stops mid-sentence; the heron is perched on the weathervane. He stares up at the immense bird. "I've seen that bird before."

"He's looking down at us," Lily says. "Maybe it wants to come in." Eventually, the sparrows resume their chatter.

"When he wants a treat, he heads into our backyard."

"Before it showed up …" Will continues.

"Harry," Joe corrects.

"Before *Harry* showed up, I was asking you what the letters mean."

"He's getting to that," Lily says softly.

"Yes. They're letters: a, i, e." He points to each letter on his change purse. "They are espies."

"Espies?"

"As in S. P." Joe draws the letters and dots in the air. "Superpower. You can call them superpowers if you want but espy rolls off the tongue easier. The 'a' stands for attention."

"Attention? A superpower?" Will asks. "As in how to pay attention?"

"And without training, we flail."

"Attention?" Will repeats, pretending to pay closer attention.

"You know how to pay attention?" Joe asks.

"Of course."

"Stand up," he says, getting up from the couch. Will stands, and Joe faces him directly.

"See my hand?" Joe waves his right hand in front of Will's face.

"Yeah, that's an old trick: you're gonna hit me with your other hand." Will points at Joe's other hand. With that, Joe goes to slap him with the hand already in front of Will's face. Before he has time to even take his eyes off Joe's left hand, Will grabs Joe's right wrist, twists, and forces Joe down to his knees.

"Woah!" Lily exclaims.

"What just happened?" Will asks, releasing Joe and helping him straighten up. "I'm sorry— did I really do that?"

"I'm not sure who else could have," Joe answers, rubbing his shoulder.

"But how? I'm not athletic or anything."

"Maybe you do know how to pay attention."

"I've never done anything like that before."

"There's a first time for everything!"

"Hey, do you hear that?" Will says.

"I don't hear anything," Lily says.

"Exactly. The sparrows have gone quiet again." Up through the skylight, the heron has cocked his long neck and meets Will's gaze. It opens its wings. A flap gives it enough buoyancy to drift. Its feet slide along the glass, and with one more flap, he lifts higher. Pulling his legs up, he flies towards the backyard.

"Time for treats," Joe says, pointing to the backdoor.

Not waiting for anyone else, Will heads to the door.

"I need to bring out sardines, or else Harry will go for the fish," Joe tells Lily. "I'll be right out."

Will opens the back door as the heron glides down to a small fishpond in the middle of the backyard. Will exits the house and heads slowly down the stone steps until he gets to flat ground. The heron turns his head sideways and looks straight at Will with one of his yellow eyes.

Lily and Joe watch from inside.

With a flap of his great wings—nearly seven feet tip to tip— the bird lifts off, barely clearing the short hedge separating the fishpond from where Will stands—and touches down on the grass not far from him. Will holds his breath so as not to spook the bird. It takes one gangly step towards him and another. Standing well over four feet tall, Will doesn't have to look down much to keep eye contact with this regal creature. The heron is close enough that Will can make out finer details: its yellow eye is complemented by the majestic black stripe atop its head and a single black ponytail of a feather.

Trust.

Will looks around the garden. Only he and the bird are present.

We worry about you.

Am I dreaming?

No …

Why can I hear you?

Telepathy.

But you're a bird.

Are birds not supposed to have thoughts?

But you're speaking English … and why is a bird speaking English?

How else would you understand me?

No, this is too weird. Will turns to leave.

If you leave, how will you ever know the truth?

Will marches up to the bird. It lowers its beak so their eyes meet.

Who are you?

A messenger. We can't save you. You need to do the saving yourself.

Who's we?

We are your friends.

Where's my father?

"Hello, Harry!" Joe says, popping open the sardine can. "I've been so wrapped up in my own species lately that I haven't made the time to talk to you."

Lily pulls Will aside as Joe holds out a sardine for the heron.

"Are you okay?"

"The bird … it can talk …"

"What?"

The heron slowly leans forward, easing its open beak towards the treat. Joe extends more, and Harry carefully moves his beak closer and plucks the sardine from Joe's hand.

"Who wants to try?"

"I do … ewww." Lily winces as she grabs a slimy bird treat.

"Take the can. It's almost empty. I'll get another." Joe hands Lily the sardine can and heads into the house.

"Hey Harry," she says softly, "look what I have for you."

Harry's beak looms over the sardine, and gingerly snatches it from her fingertips. He swallows it in a single gulp, bobbing his head.

Open your wings, Will thinks. *If you can hear me and understand me, really spread your wings.*

The bird gives his wings a quick flap.

You can do better than that. Open them wide.

The bird lowers his head and preens his chest, his neck forming an elegant curl.

That's what I thought. Coincidence.

Do you want a performance, or would you rather ask a question?

Okay … tell me something I don't know.

She wants you to kiss her.

Lily grabs the last sardine. "Your turn," Lily says, holding the fish out for Will.

Will's eyes are drawn to her lips. He takes a step towards her, grabs her shoulders in his hands, clamps his eyes shut, puckers his lips tight to brace for impact, and kisses her straight on the lips. Will opens his eyes and pulls back.

A gust of air from Harry's wings lightly lifts Lily's hair as the heron flies low and lands nearby.

"Oohkaay," Lily says, pulling away.

Will feels his face plunging three shades of deeper red. He darts towards the house. Lily's voice trails in his ear.

"Will? … wait …"

He stops and watches Lily, the girl he gave his first kiss to, toss a sardine into the air.

"Harry, catch!"

Harry snatches the sardine in midair. Lily is perfect at everything. What could she possibly see in him? He resumes his retreat.

"Will …" Lily calls to him.

Dodging Joe on the steps, Will avoids making eye contact.

"Everything okay, Will?" Joe asks, but Will disappears into the house. Lily races after him.

Making his way through Joe's house to the front door feels like a marathon. Rushing down the front steps, all he wanted to do was hide in a closet. How could he kiss Lily like that?

"Hey! Will! Stop!" Lily pleads, standing on the top front step. He can feel her eyes watching him as he marches to his bike. He looks at the cable around their bikes, one more embarrassing entanglement for Lily to witness.

Please, please, please.

With one tug, the cable slips through their bikes, freeing him for a quick escape. He hops on and places his foot on the pedal. His bike lurches forward, but he stops when Lily grabs him by the forearm. She is strong, chipped pinky nail polish and all; he likes it.

"What was that? You kissed me!"

"I shouldn't have done that."

"I'm not complaining. I don't understand why you kissed me

… Joe saw it."

"Harry told me to."

"Harry, the bird?"

"Ah, never mind."

"I can't *never mind* that one. Harry told you to kiss me?"

"While I was standing there in front of the heron someone …
or something … was having a conversation with me. Harry
said you wanted me to kiss you. Look, this is all a big mistake.
Can we pretend that didn't happen?"

"No, we can't." Her face softens. "I *did* want you to kiss me,
but … not in front of Joe …"

"Wait. You did?"

Lily's face flushes. "Yeah … but I wanted our first kiss to be
private."

"I'm sorry."

"You're sorry you kissed me?"

"No! That's not what I meant. I'm sorry I spoiled our first
kiss. You're right, as usual. It should have been private."

"You didn't spoil it. Actually, it was kind of special in a funny
way. You kissed me while I was holding a sardine."

"What a first kiss story."

"That was your first kiss?"

"Yeah … was it yours?"

"Yeah." Lily collects her bike. They walk on the inside of their
bikes. "If we ever get married, this'll be the funny story we tell
our kids."

"Yeah … but can we not tell our kids?"

o o o

"Mom!" Will slams the door behind him, checking the kitchen and dining room. "Mom?" He hollers up the stairs.

"I'm out back!"

Following the trail of her voice, Will rushes through the house and out the side door. He finds her standing in the middle of a brush pile, holding a rake. His father's college sweatshirt hangs off her petite body. His throat, tightening from burgeoning tears, renders him speechless. She drops the rake and rushes to him. Unable to move his feet, he raises his arms. His mother's arms pull him in and press firmly against his back. He squeezes back and buries his face in her shoulder. His tears moisten his father's sweatshirt. The reminder of his father releases a flood of tears. His fingers claw and grip the sweatshirt's soft, bulky material. He is being held by his mother and father, but in that moment, he can't decide if he wants his father or hates him.

"Oh, sweetie, what is it?"

"Am I gonna go crazy like Dad?" He lifts his head to face her; his eyes are swollen with tears.

"What? Where did you hear that?"

"Uncle Rod. He always talks about Dad being crazy."

"No, don't even think it. Your Uncle Rod has no filter. He can be a real douche sometimes."

"Mom, language."

"Well, he can be. Good intentions and all, he can be a DB." She sits down on the loveseat swing and taps the seat next to her. Will joins her.

"You were only four years old. You were there, but you couldn't understand. Heck, I couldn't. It was all so crazy—shit! Sorry, language. It was all so unbelievable." She turns to him. "Look at me. Your father did not go crazy, and neither will you."

"Mom, I owe you an apology."

"For what?"

"I never believed you."

Her face flushes.

"You're right. I was there. I remember some things; not everything, but enough. Your story … it always made sense, crazy sense, but sense. I just … I didn't want to believe it. I think I didn't want to believe it because it's scary. No, not scary … more than that … *terrifying*."

His mother holds back tears. "Yes. It was truly frightening." She places his hand in hers. "And to think those men are still out there and what they might have done … yup … terrifying." A tear flows down her cheek.

"This is crazy, right? It doesn't add up. I want a life where everything makes sense," Will sighs. "In a messed-up way, it was easier to believe Dad was a dirtbag and left us than the other story."

"Your dad was a lot of things," she smiles, "but dirtbag wasn't one of them."

"I think what I'm most upset about is you were trying to tell me all along, and I didn't want to believe it. I made up this story, this lie, to convince myself, because as bad as it was, it was easier than the truth. I'm sorry. I thought you were crazy."

He scans her face. Tears well up in her eyes.

"If the choice is between a crazy mom and a dirtbag dad, I'd rather you think your mom is crazy."

"It wasn't just that I thought it, I *built* a picture of you as crazy," Will says, wiping away a tear. "I *made* you that way."

"Honestly, there were times I thought I was going crazy. Some mornings I can hear your father saying …"

"Wake up."

"Yes. Exactly. Wake up."

Will leans in. She wraps her arm around him then wipes a tear from her cheek. "Will,"

"Yeah?"

"This is some crazy shit."

"Mom, language. There's a kid here." Will snickers and smiles; he settles into his mother's embrace.

"And that's just it. You're not a kid anymore," she sighs.

"Mom,"

"Yeah?"

"I kissed Lily."

NINE

Will the Real Oscar Please Stand?

Will knocks on the door behind Mr. Bohr's desk.

"Oh, good morning Will," Mr. Bohr says, opening the door. "You're early!"

"Good morning, Mr. Bohr. Do you have time for a physics question?"

"Perhaps you can ask it during class so everyone can hear?"

"Well, this one's about stuff that won't be on the finals."

"How do you know what's on the finals?"

"It's about a quantum wave's collapse to a point particle during observation."

"Oh, well, in that case, you already know the answer."

"Huh?"

"That's the answer to the extra credit question on the final; no need to worry, you've got it. Don't go blabbing it."

"But I haven't gotten to my question yet."

"I guess I jumped the gun. Shoot," Mr. Bohr chuckles.

"Do physicists know why observation causes a field of potential to collapse to a particle?"

"I don't cover things I can't explain."

"Don't you think that's a problem? Why stop there? Why not cover those things that we can't explain? Don't you think that might get us excited? Speak to near-death experiencers like Allie's mom. Bring us spoon benders. Show us pictures of flying saucers. Take us to a haunted house. Then tell us future scientists to explain it."

"Is that a rhetorical question, or do you really want me to answer?"

"Yeah, no, I wanted to talk about my first question. I think it's strange."

"Yes, it's a mystery."

"But it's not the same kind of mystery as discoveries like centrifugal force, or pulleys, or even electricity. It's a much stranger mystery than any of those. It's *observation* that causes the collapse, right?"

"That seems to be the case, yes."

"Any kind of observation?"

"There's only so many ways one can observe the subatomic world, but from what we can tell, yes, any kind of observation."

"See? That's strange. What's linking them?"

"Are you going somewhere with this?"

"What if consciousness is the link? What if consciousness is causing the field of potential to make a decision?"

"Hold on, Will. Particles can't decide anything."

"Well, something picked one spot from a cloud of possible locations."

"You're anthropomorphizing, talking like atoms are alive." Mr. Bohr adjusts his glasses. "That's highly speculative territory."

"Haven't all discoveries started with speculation?"

"It takes a lot more than that to discover something."

"But that's where they all start, don't they? Isn't the birthplace of all discoveries when someone wonders about something? When they wonder about something they don't know the answer to?"

He motions to Will to come all the way into the back room and closes the door. "You're a smart kid; I'll be straight with you." Mr. Bohr leans in and lowers his voice. "You start down that path and half the world will call you a flake; the other half will say you're spreading the word of the devil. Watch who you say things like that to. The world is better with you in it."

o o o

Lily grabs her lunch tray and scans the cafeteria. Allie is eating by herself; she smiles invitingly as other girls from their class pass by and cluster at another table. Lily checks the room again, sighs, and heads to Allie.

"Mind if I sit here?"

Allie slides her things towards her to make sure Lily has enough room. Lily quietly sets down her tray. She arranges her food and utensils, avoiding eye contact. Allie takes a drink of water and stares into her lap. "I want to apologize…"

"Thanks."

Allie puts down her drink and picks up her taco with both hands, inspecting it for freshness. She glances at Lily. "So, how's things with Will?"

"Well," she meets Allie's eyes. "He kissed me."

"Get out of here!" Allie drops her taco on her tray.

Lily busts out, smiling ear to ear.

"Spill."

"Hey Lily," Sarah says, stopping by their table. "Mind if I sit with you?"

"Uh, sure," Lily says. Sarah sets her tray in front of an empty stool and takes her seat.

"And look at you, getting some. Good for you," Sarah tells Lily.

"What?"

Behind Lily's back, Allie runs her finger across her throat to kill the conversation.

"Who told you that?" Lily's heart pounds harder as her face grows warm.

Sarah flashes her eyes at Allie. "You know. … Will she or won't she?" Allie glares at Sarah. "Wait, was I not supposed to know that?" Her face freezes in a cringe. "Sheesh, Allie, and you wonder why nobody likes you. I'm sorry, Lily." Sarah collects her tray. "Good luck with Will," she says to Lily and heads for another table.

"You told her? I confided in you! You said you were my bestie!"

"Don't get your panties in a bunch. People say 'You're my bestie.' like 'How's it going?' or 'Have a nice day.'"

"Allie! I told you that in confidence. And what's with the 'Will she or won't she' crap?"

Allie twirls her ponytail with a finger. "I may have embellished a bit."

"What did you say?"

"I may have said you were thinking about hooking up with Will."

"Allie! Now that lie's gonna travel, and everybody's gonna think I'm a slut."

"That will help your odds with Rich."

"UUUUGGGHHH. I can't believe you."

"Okay, I may have screwed up. I'm still your friend. Can you tell me the kiss story?"

"Best friends don't divulge secrets." Lily gets up and wipes tears from her cheek. "Have a nice day," she scowls and walks away.

"Lily!" Allie calls after her.

"You deserved that," a girl crows from behind, her asymmetrical green and blue bob concealing her left eye and revealing multiple piercings in her right ear. "You're devoid of empathy."

"Are you hitting on me, Ivy?"

"Ugh! You're so what's wrong with the world. My *type* is

anyone with *compassion*; that rules you out," Ivy says and walks away.

By herself, Allie reassembles her taco. "I really wanted to hear that kiss story."

∘ ∘ ∘

"I was hoping to give you a tour of our backyard yesterday," Joe says, "but Harry had his own plans. Come with me." They head out back to where they were yesterday. A man-made stream bisects the yard, terminating in a central fishpond. Will follows Lily, pointing at each koi she spots, as she crosses over stone steps peaking above the water.

"Harry's observant. We only brought them out last week," Joe says.

Stepping down past the pond, the sand-colored pea gravel path crunches under their feet. Sunlight dances between and through luminescent leaves, dappling the earth below. Light and summery clouds drift by. Joe takes a seat on the grass. Will and Lily join him under the tree.

"Joe?"

"Yes, Will?"

"Have you ever heard of wave-particle duality?"

"Sure."

"Ever thought about it? Isn't it strange?"

"Yes, I thought about it; and yes, it is, and no, it isn't strange."

"Is that like the sound of one hand clapping?"

"Haha, no, it's much simpler than that. It's strange until you understand it, and then it's just normal. The thought that you could listen to someone from three towns over—no wires in between—would've sounded strange before radio was invented. Now it's just the way it is. It's boring even."

"But it's a mystery."

"It's about to stop being a mystery. Science is on the verge of discovering yet another realm that runs by its own set of rules: consciousness. They are dipping their toes in the water, and that water is dark and deep."

"Yeah, that's what I was wondering about. Is *consciousness* doing something to cause waves to become particles?"

"We've known for a long time that observing the world changes it, but scientists don't know what to do with that. Those who are pushing into these new frontiers are being disrespected by those who feel threatened by the idea that observing the world changes it. It reminds me of men who refused to look into Galileo's telescope. Things haven't changed much … yet."

"Why wouldn't people want to know?"

"Within each of us lies tremendous power; power to topple those who are in power today. You think they want the people of the world to wake up to their own superpowers?—not a chance. You think the discovery of electricity was big? This is bigger. Compared to what's to come, bending spoons might as well be a parlor trick."

A trio of crows glides overhead and lands at a box feeder.

"Don't you want to shoo them away?" Will says. "They'll eat

all the bird food."

"Isn't that what it's for? Crows are smart … friendly even. Not too many people like crows. I don't know why."

"I like crows," Lily says.

"They can teach you a lot about yourself. Crows are shapeshifters; they can be both here and there at once. They can see the past, present, and future simultaneously because time is an illusion.

"When a crow presents itself to you, it is an omen of change. Crow is asking you to pay attention. Your observation will determine what needs to shift, so you can shape your future." Joe shuts an eye tight to keep the sun out.

"Isn't that superstition?" Will says. "They're just crows."

"How do you define superstition?"

"Crows are crows; that's all. All the other stuff is nonsense. It's not real."

"Hey crows, are you real?" They take off.

"Of course they're real."

"Are you real?"

"Duh, yeah."

Lily nods, too.

"How do you know?"

"I can feel myself," Will says, grabbing his arm.

Joe nods. "Your five senses are there because of your consciousness. Consciousness is one of the universe's invisible forces. You don't end at your fingertips. Your consciousness extends beyond your physical body. Attention, intention, and expectation … these create the shift."

"I don't understand," Will says.

"Putting your attention on something is like pointing a finger at it. The invisible energy of your intention leaves the tip of your finger and connects to the thing you're pointing at. Expectation is how you think it will turn out. When your intention and your expectation become one, that's when you experience your true power."

"I thought physics was hard. You're making me crazy," Will says.

"Get used to that feeling, we're just getting started." Joe pats the grass. "Today is a day to watch the clouds go by." He lies back to take in the sky.

Lily drops, comfortable and satisfied, onto the grass as if it were her bed. Will leans back awkwardly on his elbows, eventually lying down all the way. The tender, sun-warmed grass feels good on his back.

"Look at them slowly drifting by," Joe says. "Watch long enough, and you'll see some emerge from out of the blue, others fade away. Thoughts behave similarly. What would it be like if you could sit back and observe your thoughts as they come and go, the same way you're watching these clouds go by?"

"Watch my thoughts?" Lily asks.

"There is a chatterbox in our head, and sometimes it distracts us, adds to our stress, and doesn't do much else. Learn how to quiet it. When you observe your chatterbox, it settles down."

"I know what this is," Lily chimes in eagerly. "It's meditation!"

"Yes! Meditation is good for your *attention,* and it can help quiet your automatic, impulsive, critical thoughts so you can hear the other ones better. Try this: Notice your breath. Notice each inhale and notice each exhale. If a thought arises, notice it the same way you notice a cloud in the sky. And when you do that, notice if it evaporates."

Will rolls his head to look at Lily. Her eyes are closed.

Inhale.

Exhale.

Will opens his eyes to see what's crawling up his wrist. He gently scoots the ladybug off his wrist and resumes.

Inhale.

Exhale.

Will opens his eyes again. This time the ladybug has landed on his other arm. He blows the ladybug off his arm and resumes.

Inhale.

Exhale.

Lily peeks an eye at Joe, her arm raised to keep the sun out of her face. "My mind keeps wandering."

"This ladybug kept landing on me; I couldn't focus."

"Good."

"Good?" Will asks. "But we both failed." Lily nods in agreement.

"You didn't fail. You're learning how your mind works. You

got to see how distractible you are. Think of it like this," Joe motions to his body. "We each live in a spaceship that's powered by thought. As the pilot, we need to stay alert, or we'll fly right into the side of a mountain. That moment when you catch yourself daydreaming or ruminating? That's waking up. Easier said than done, so we practice.

"Waking up?" Will sits up. "I hear my dad saying that to me all the time ...."

Joe props himself on an elbow to face Will. "Constipation of the brain ... unclench." Joe taps Will on his forehead. "Let all the crap out." Lily giggles. "Ego makes shit and holds on to it ... shithead," Joe says.

"Huh?"

"That's what I named the negative voice in my head: shithead. Reminds me that I'm not him. Whenever he shows up, I say, 'Hey, shithead. I'm not listening to you today.' Wanna name yours?"

"Oscar."

Joe chuckles. "The Grouch. Good one. Lily, how about ..."

"Allie," she says, scrunching her face.

"Hello, Oscar. Hello, Allie. Nice to meet you," Joe says.

"Here's a question: Who's running your train of thought? You? Or Oscar? Or Allie? You don't need to answer that. Just something to think about." He starts back towards the house. "Once Oscar is in control, you aren't."

o o o

Will slips into bed.

Joe said to focus on the breath, so here goes.

Inhale.

Exhale.

Inhale.

Exhale.

Inhale.

Exhale.

Will rolls onto his stomach and burps, releasing the aroma of zesty, half-digested pepperoni pizza.

Inhale.

Exhale.

Inhale.

Exhale.

A sliver of pink light on the horizon indicates dawn is not far off. Like chugging locomotives, billows of Will and Lily's breath hang in the air behind them as they run across the open field.

Crack! Crunch!

Will whips his head around, hoping to catch a glimpse of the assailant. All he can make out is a dark, fast-approaching blur.

"Come on! He's coming!" Will grabs Lily's hand. The tall grass shushes beneath their feet. Will makes out the outline of a gazebo in the distance.

"There! Run! Go! Go! Go!" He pushes her away.

"What are you doing?"

"Go get help!"

"I'm not leaving you."

Will pulls out a hunting knife.

"Where did you get that?"

"It doesn't matter. I can use this to slow him down."

"Are you crazy! You're going to kill yourself. Is that what you want?"

"No more running! He's just going to keep coming until I face him."

"Oh no. Will …" Lily gasps and steps back, pointing. "Don't hurt him."

The field falls silent. Will slowly turns his head. The figure is behind him, close enough to stab. The waning moon behind his assailant casts him as a silhouette. His oversize hoodie cloaks his face in shadow.

"I'm not afraid of you anymore! Show yourself!" Will yells, brandishing his knife. The glint of moonlight off the blade flashes on the assailant's face, revealing only his nose and lips.

"Come on!" Will hollers, jabbing the knife at the assailant. Will's demand is met with silence. The figure takes a defiant step towards Will.

"It's you and me, Oscar."

"Oscar? Who's the one holding the knife?"

"Show yourself!"

The figure extends his open palms. "I don't need weapons. What are you trying to prove, Oscar?"

"I'm not Oscar!" Will jabs the knife at his assailant's belly. The assailant dodges the knife and clutches Will's knife hand. With a quick, assertive twist, the assailant forces Will to drop the knife and brings Will to his knees.

"Is this what you want? Aren't you tired of fighting?" He twists Will's wrist harder and presses a hand against Will's shoulder. Will struggles to free himself. "Get off me! Get off me!"

"What are you afraid of?"

His assailant's warm breath blows on the back of his neck. His breath smells of pepperoni.

"I want you to just leave me alone!"

The assailant releases him and steps back. Gripping his sore shoulder, Will scrambles to his feet to face him. A breeze rustles autumn leaves as it passes through the trees; like tiny ballerinas, silken milkweed tutus flit around them.

Will rushes his assailant, knocking them both to the ground.

"Show me who you are!" Will yanks the hoodie back. The silvery moonlight reveals his twin staring back at him. However, his eyes are soft. His stare is confident.

"Look," his twin says.

An immense shadow envelops them. Milkweed stalks rattle and quiver. Vibrations reverberate up through the ground into his knees and up Will's spine. The hairs on his arms stand up. The ionized air reminds him of the feeling before a thunderstorm. A deep hum dominates the soundscape. He looks up, but instead of a storm cloud, moving slowly and silently, Will sees a giant change purse. It blots out the blue-black sky.

"Wake up, Oscar." With a shove from his twin, Will falls backward off a cliff. As he free-falls and flails, he turns in time to watch the ground rushing to meet him.

THUD!

"Will, are you okay?"

Will looks up from the floor beside his bed and sees his mother's silhouette in the frame of his door.

"I'm fine. I'm fine."

PART TWO

INTO DARKNESS

TEN

Welcome to The A.U.

"PRAY FOR GOD to give you something important to do."

From a Hopi Prophecy

"William Freeman … man of the hour."

Keeping his hand on his car door, Bill turns to face a broad-shouldered man in a finely tailored black suit and matching fedora. "Have we met?"

Mary turns from buckling WJ into his booster seat. "Billy, it's starting to rain."

"Ma'am,"—he tips his hat at Mary—"I need to borrow your husband for one minute … if you don't mind."

"Billy? …"

"It's okay Mary; get in the car. We'll be just a minute. I want to tell Mr. Krone what we decided."

Mary double-checks WJ's straps, shuts the door, and walks around the car to the front passenger seat.

The suited man tugs at his cuffs. "Why did you stop answering your phone? Mr. Krone doesn't like it when people don't pick up."

"I don't want to have this conversation."

"He made you a generous offer."

"I know, I know, and I appreciate the offer."

"You've charmed him." He leans in and murmurs, "As one con man to another, I'm impressed." A crude tattoo of a black cross peeks out above the left side of his crisp white collar. Bill glances at the other car in the parking lot, a shiny black SUV, engine still running. As the tinted rear window rolls up he catches a glimpse of Mr. Krone's unmistakable thick glasses balanced on his ski ridge of a nose. "I wish you well in your talent search … but I'm not interested. Now if you'll excuse me, I have to get my family home."

The suited man grabs Bill's arm. Under the man's right ear, Bill makes out a more elaborate tattoo: a dark angel, a scale in one hand, a sword in the other. Each of the fingers on his right hand is tattooed with a black letter spelling F-E-A-R.

"You can accept Mr. Krone's offer, or he can have you committed."

"He can't do that."

"You want to find out?"

"Let go of me!" Bill jerks his arm free, gets in the car, and locks the door.

"What's going on?" Mary asks.

"You're making a mistake," the man threatens, his breath fogging Bill's window. "Talk some sense into your husband. He's passing up the offer of a lifetime; you'd be rich!"

Bill starts the car and steps hard on the gas. Tires screech as he heads towards the exit. He checks the side-view mirror; the suited man is rushing back to the other car.

"Who was that? … Billy, slow down! WJ is in the back seat." Bill takes a sharp right.

"It's a long story … not now."

Up ahead, brooding storm clouds approach.

"What's going on? What offer was he talking about? When we get home I need the full story …"

"We're not going home." The tires screech again as he takes the corner.

"Slow down. You crossed the line. Please."

"I need to tell you something."

"What?"

Screech!

"I'm a star seed."

"What? Oh my God. You know what the doctor said: you can't just go off your meds."

"That's not it … they're after me, Mary." He checks the rearview mirror.

"I thought we agreed there's no such thing."

"You did; I didn't. They want me because I'm a star seed."

"You're scaring WJ. Pull over and let me drive."

"I'm not psychotic … I'm psychic."

"I'm a cycloptic sidekick," WJ giggles.

"Mary, don't poison him against me."

"Those were your words, not mine." Her voice grows stern.

"I have abilities. I'm not going to deny it anymore. They want me because of my abilities."

She shakes her head. "No … stop it! Mira and Joe are filling your head with New Age nonsense."

"I love you Mary, but I'm right about this." He looks in the side-view mirror. "And those men chasing us are proof."

Sheets of rain quickly obscure visibility. Bill turns the wipers on fast. Their tires carve channels in the standing water on the road. Bill takes the bend in the road too wide. The high beams of the pursuing car blinds him; he flips the rearview mirror to night mode.

"Are you nuts?"

I'm not crazy."

Screech!

"Slow down! You crossed the line again! You're going to get us all killed! Billy—Jesus!"

Screech!

Light floods the car's interior.

"TOO BRIGHT!" WJ calls out.

"WJ, cover your eyes for Mommy! Don't uncover them until I let go of your shoe." Mary's fingers press into the toe of his right sneaker.

Bill swerves the car hard to the right, pressing WJ's shoulder into the rear driver's side door.

"You're going too fast, Billy! You can't see … turn off the high beams. The rain is making it worse!"

"That's not our high beams. That's theirs."

Bang! The car slams into them.

"What the hell! Oh my God, Billy! Hold on WJ."

"I'm sorry, I brought this upon us …."

"Look out!" Mary screams.

Something immense glides over the hood. A wing swipes the rain from the windshield. Billy jerks the wheel to the right to avoid the creature.

The interior goes dark. The high beams suddenly disappear.

"What was that?" Mary says.

"A bird."

"Birds don't fly in storms!"

"That one does!"

Mary looks back. "Billy, they're gone. Hold on WJ, we're almost home."

"No, they're not. I know them."

"No," she studies the road behind them. "They're not there. Where did they go?" Mary releases WJ's sneaker. "They're gone. I don't see them. Oh my god, Billy, the bird is still here!"

"I'd rather a bird than them."

"Why won't they leave us alone? You told them no, didn't you?"

"It's because I told them no."

Vvvrrowm. The car jostles to the right.

"What was that!"

"I told you …. Mary, if anything happens to me …."

"No!…"

"… promise me."

"Billy, stop it!…"

"You have to promise me!"

Vvvrrowmmmmmmmmm!

"What?!"

"Tell Mira!" Bill swerves to the left to regain control of the car.

"It's loud Mama! Make it go away!"

"WJ … hold on!" Mary claws the air for WJ's shoe.

VVVRROWMMMMMMMMM!

The energetic push is too much. Bill loses control, and the car heads down a ditch towards a cluster of saplings.

Bang!

The airbags deploy. WJ is crying. Mary is slumped over her airbag.

Bill glances in the rearview mirror.

"Mary!" He shakes her shoulder. "Mary …"

She whimpers and moans. She's alive.

Bill hears footfalls on gravel. They are coming. His hands fumble beneath his airbag. He finds the horn and presses hard.

"Mary! God … help us!"

"Billy, what's happening?" She lifts her face. Blood oozes from a crack on the bridge of her nose.

"Oh my God! Mary, you're bleeding …" Frantically, he tries to open the door, but a tree blocks the way.

The car slumps down in front with a metallic *crunch*. The

suited man, soaking wet, is on the hood. He gets on all fours, his face inches from the wipers. He rips the wiper off and pulls back a meaty fist with brass knuckles.

The windshield shatters like a wave crashing, sudden and loud, against 10,000 tiny bells. Mary screams and shields her face as glass shards pepper the interior.

The suited man yanks at the smashed windshield and peels the driver's side away. He grabs something from his jacket pocket then leans in through the opening.

"No! No! No! No! Mary, run!"

"Billy! No!" Mary screams at the sight of the man's knife.

The suited man restrains Bill with his right arm. Mary swats at him defensively while he slices through the seatbelt.

He grabs Bill with both hands and pulls hard on Bill's arms. Bill tries to resist, but the suited man pulls Bill up and out of the car, dragging the right side of Bill's face along the sharp edges of smashed glass. Bill yelps from the searing pain on his cheek.

The suited man studies the bloody, messy gash. "You just earned your wings." He tosses Bill off the hood. "Welcome to the A.U."

Super Human

ELEVEN

Mr. E

Bill opens his eyes and looks at the clock on the nightstand; it reads 11:11. *WJ! I saw him!* He throws off his covers and swings his legs over the side of the bed. His bare feet touching the hardwood floor wakes him up to the day's cold reality. "Shower on … 102 degrees," his voice echoes off the Carrara marble walls and floor of his bathroom. The shower complies. He disrobes and steps into his spacious tomb of glass, marble, and gold fittings. He grabs at the shelf for his electric shaver; miscalculating his wet grip, it tumbles to the shower floor with a clatter. He picks it up and stands, letting the water massage his back.

Age and anger have turned his face gaunt; time has stamped crow's feet firmly beside his eyes. His full, brown hair Mary loved running her fingers through has started to gray. He studies his scarred cheek in the fogging mirror in front of him. The contrast of his embarrassing scar and this glorious luxury apartment strikes him. He's only here because he intervened on his own behalf; interfered is more like it. His refusal to cooperate with their demands was met with fierce punishment. His face disappears in the fogged mirror, a man erased.

Bill wipes the mirror. *I'm still here.* A vision of WJ putting on his black belt flashes in the mirror. He smiles.

He got my message.

He stretches to let the sleep out of him. In his oversized shower, he can stretch his arms out in any direction and still have room to move. His shower is larger and more elegant than the cold cell where they kept him for seven years. Unlike his clouded reflection, his first days of imprisonment remain vivid. The only light came through a slit sized to pass a food tray at the base of a wall. With that faint illumination, he could make out a cot and a toilet. Reaching to find the perimeter of his surroundings, he felt the cold, clammy stone walls. Between groping like a blind man and letting his eyes adjust, he discovered his cell was larger than arms' reach but only barely.

How long was he there? It was hard to tell. He had two measures of time. One measure was the growth of his hair. It would grow out, then one day he would wake up and it would be gone. Like a lion in the wild, he was gassed while he slept, treated, and returned. All these precautions were unnecessary. They were the beasts. They were the predators—except these predators chased money and power; he was chasing the truth.

Another way he measured time was when they would bring him to just enough to ask him if he was ready to cooperate. His answer was always the same: "I will not violate the Law of Free Will." How many times did they ask that? A hundred? More? In solitary confinement, he had only his mind to keep him company … and occasionally Mira. They conversed telepathically, though he can't be sure of any of that. Deprived of light, he had countless hallucinations. On more than one occasion, she visited him, he likes to think since she told him teleportation comes naturally to those like her. She radiated beauty and reassurance, buoying his spirit. She could have broken him out easily, but she reminded him that within hardship is the opportunity to learn something about oneself. Look for the lesson. Maintain nonjudgmental awareness. Have compassion for his captors. He was not the one imprisoned. "Use this time to deepen your practice," she advised. "In your heart of hearts, how do you want this to turn out?"

How he longed to be with his family again. Countless times he tried contacting Mary and WJ telepathically, both while he was awake and in his dreams. He had no idea if they received any of his messages. Today felt different.

After one gassing, he awoke to find himself in a new cell: still small; still cold, clammy stone; still a wall slit, cot, and toilet; but the food tray slit had changed. Crouching low to get a better look, he could see a clear plexiglass airlock.

Hermetically sealed food trays were delivered by drones. The buzz from the approaching fans and the hiss and clicks of the airlock alerted him to mealtime. Hi remote viewing skills let him see the full extent of this prison: his stone cell, wrapped in lead, was suspended inside a massive silo at least a mile underground. An array of golden lights—each could contain a basketball—crisscrossed its inner surface.

Not only were they imprisoning him, but they were entombing his exhalations, every cell he shed. The reasons they kept him here were clear to him: it was to create paranoia.

In their ignorance, they presumed all these layers of protection would ensure that he could not reach them. This elaborate prison was comical. They were *terrified* of him. He was trained in attention, intention, and expectation—the most potent weapons ever devised. What else could reveal lies without drugs? What else could topple tyrants without firing a single shot?

The multi-layered confinement was useless. Consciousness was connected to every point in space and time. No material barrier, no planet's crust could stop it.

"Hello Bill," was how Mira liked to announce her arrival.

"Hi Mira, have a seat," he would tap beside him on the cot.

"You are well protected here. A sizable vein of black tourmaline runs around the abandoned mine shaft and chamber. Their hateful energies can't penetrate it."

"Mira, you said this was all for a reason. What is it?"

"If I told you, it wouldn't have the same impact." Mira was often like that, withholding information until the moment was right. "But I will say this … this is an opportunity for you to practice waking up."

After his refusal to train others on how to grow within them the gift that he was given, they put him in the hole. Cooperation was incomprehensible to him because their purpose was not for the greater good; they were driven by greed and power.

The term was remote influencing, psychically affecting people's feelings and thoughts at a distance. Mira cautioned him on this front: "It's one thing to be persuasive; it's another thing to be manipulative."

Thus, he remained steadfast. He kept up his mental practices, meditating on loving-kindness. Year after year, it kept him sane. He used his psychic abilities to plead his case to Mr. Krone: show mercy! But Mr. Krone was immune to such appeals. The flesh is weak, and the grinding passage of time took its toll on Bill.

His final words to Mira remained etched in his mind. He asked her, "What should I do?"

"You have a *very* special gift and the free will to use it, Bill Freeman."

"I'm using my gifts, and I'm still stuck here."

"Are you sure that you're using all of them?"

"Can't you just tell me what I'm missing?"

"I've said it before …."

"… if I told you, it wouldn't have the same impact," Bill
finished her sentence.

"I have taught you as best I can. Your education is now in
your hands. Your next steps are for you and you alone to
choose. It is time to let experience and your own choices
guide you."

Freeman … the irony.

He knew Mira was right but wanted a second opinion. He
appealed to a higher source: he pleaded to God for an answer.
When none came, he knew he had to figure it out on his
own.

What harm could it possibly be if he manipulated his captors
to do what was morally right and put an end to his unjust
imprisonment? Surely, a loving God would show mercy for
this sin, if it could even be called a sin! These people were
incurring their own karmic debt, it would benefit them too to
put an end to this. He would be helping them! Just this one
time he could put an end to this tragic injustice, this tortured
existence.

He knew Mr. Krone was immune to pleas for empathy,
compassion, and mercy. He saw those emotions as flawed, as
weaknesses. There were already too many people on the
planet; mercy kept those around who'd forfeited their right to
exist by virtue of their stupidity. Mr. Krone could only be
plied by appeals to power. Mr. Krone was prone to daydream
when he was happiest, when he was counting his money. That
was also when he was most vulnerable to psychic

manipulation.

"I'm spending all this money to let a good apple rot," he muttered.

He's draining your funds. He's winning.

"Two-hundred-billion dollars, and my best asset is locked away two miles down."

Bill's harmless. Free him. He'll make you more money.

Another ten billion...

You need more money. Free him.

I need more money.

You'll have more money. Free him.

"Free Bill, and I'll have more money."

And with that, Bill reclaimed his freedom.

"Ow!" He jerks the shaver away from his neck. He wipes the mirror; a spot of blood bubbles up. He inspects the foil. A tiny piece of metal has broken off. He looks at his reflection again. The tiny crimson droplet grows heavy under its own weight until it runs, translucent red mixing with the water on his neck.

He wipes the glass and squints through the foggy shower-misted air. His wall clock reads 11:25. He is very late. *Good. This is* my *life, dammit. I'm taking my life back.*

"Shower off," he sighs, grabs a towel, and buries his face in it. Hiding like this would be good; could he get away with it for a few years? If only there were a way to hide from his own demons; his barometer of self-worth is near empty.

Mira, how many times must I ask?

"Do you want me to beg you?" Bill talks into the mirror. Maybe his surveillance efforts will locate someone in her circles. The A.C. honeypot trap has been set and is poised to catch a fly— even the kind that might vanish if you blink.

Returning to the bedroom, he sits on his side of the bed. The wall of mirrors in front of him reflects the king-size bed and his loneliness. The side of the bed where he sleeps had been turned down, but the other where Mary should be was untouched. He purposely laid his clothes out on that side like a dismembered companion.

He scratches his finger under his A.U. ring. The gold ring's triangle-cut purple sapphire is encircled by two serpents, each eating the other's tails. This gaudy, symbolic shackle makes his skin crawl literally. The cheap gold-plated ring has been known to turn his skin blue-green, other times a flaming red itch-fest. The irony: the membership ring of a secret society run by the richest man on the planet is forged with cheap materials. He tries to pull it off, but it won't slip over his knuckle.

The promise of fresh-brewed coffee draws him out of his bedroom. Passing through the living room, he laments. Material things are such cold comfort. What good is a leather couch if you don't have a family to share it with? Ahh, to be able to breathe in the soothing lavender of Mary's hair again! To hug WJ again! To see how he's grown!

Produce results, and we'll let you go, they said. Contact *anyone* from your former life, and we kill your son, they said.

That drowning, heart-sinking feeling emerges again.

In his gleaming, minimalist kitchen of Carrera marble and austere white cabinetry, he fills his mug with lukewarm coffee, brewed when he was supposed to have woken up. He pours in the cream, and it sinks to the bottom, disappearing in the caffeinated darkness. He lowers the spoon. Lighter whorls of cream slowly swirl upward, struggling to penetrate the darkness, reminding him of his former prison.

His phone buzzes in his pocket. **Mr. Krone**, the screen reports. He turns it off, grabs his coffee, and moves to the marble-topped island. A text from Ash flashes on his phone: **Get your ass here.**

"Is it too much for me to take my time one God-damned day?" he snarls. He texts his reply: **On my way**, grabs his coffee and suit jacket, and hurries out the door with only one thought on his mind:

Get my family back.

TWELVE

Mr. Krone

"Mr. E, before you go in, there are new developments," Hack informs Bill, intercepting him in the hallway between the break room and his office. Hack hands Bill a folder. "The honeypot …"

"This is going to have to wait." Bill slaps the folder on Hack's chest.

"Sir, it can't wait," Hack says. Bill enters his office and draws the blinds to disappear, but he's already been found.

"My star seed," a gravelly voice announces. Bill turns. The glow from a cigarette lighter illuminates the arthritic hands and gaunt face of Mr. Krone and his thick glasses. With the orange glow of lit tobacco followed by a puff of smoke, he emerges from a dark corner of Bill's office.

"I was going to send you a report," Bill quickly defends.

"You've something new to say?" Mr. Krone sits in Bill's desk chair. "Because I haven't heard a word from you in months."

"I'm on the verge, I can feel it," Bill implores, maneuvering uncomfortably close to Mr. Krone to get to the microwave. He pops his coffee in, starts it, then backs away.

"You know how many times I've heard that?"

"I know … I know, but I've had new developments … sounds." Bill grabs a notepad off his desk, unclips the pen nestled in its spiral binding, and starts jotting down notes.

"Sounds?"

"Yes, the asset started making sounds. Well, I think that's the source, but they're coming from all over the hangar … very low frequency. We're even reading sonic pulses well below the audible range for humans … for anything, even wavelengths of forty-thousand kilometers. Resonances like those are of advanced meditators."

"I entrusted the most sophisticated thing humanity's ever laid eyes on to you, and all you can give me is *sounds*?"

Beep, beep, beep.

Bill ignores the microwave. "If we could direct it …"

"I suppose next you're going to tell me this thing's alive."

"No. Well … no. But, highly anomalous … I hesitated to tell you this, but …"

"I'm listening."

"It moved."

"Go on."

"I can't find the words to describe it; it blobbed like some kind of non-Newtonian fluid. Our working theory is it's MMI … mind-matter interaction."

"Bill, that's great."

"Great. Right, great," he chuckles nervously.

"You've created a middle school science project."

"No, no, this is important!"

"I think it's time we cut bait."

"That would be a bad idea. All the progress I've made. I think
…"

"You want to hear what I think? I think you think you're
special." He takes a long drag off his cigarette. "I think I can
pluck anyone off the street, and they'd do a better job than
you."

Beep, beep, beep.

"This is not a job you can hand to just anyone. This is no
toy."

"I remember when I believed in you. That time has passed.
But we both know the truth now, don't we Bill? You're a
fraud." Mr. Krone comes out from behind the desk. "You'd
be less pathetic if you admitted it; your cot's waiting for you."

"You wouldn't do that."

"You don't know me, Bill." He steps right up to Bill. "You'd
never see the light of day again."

"But you promised …"

"All bets are off. I wouldn't be a good sportsman if I didn't
give the fox a head start; you've got until the end of the
week."

"Give me my family back."

"Excuse me?"

"Give me my family back, and I'll do it. I can't do it without them."

"Why should I listen to the man who failed to deliver on his promise to make me more money?"

Bill stops taking notes.

"He's draining your funds. He's winning," Mr. Krone mocks.

Bill drops his pen.

"What? Did you think you had me fooled? Amateur. I'm one of the good guys." Mr. Krone takes a drag off his cigarette.

"Let me prove to you how good I can be. Get this open, and you can have them back."

"Are you being serious?"

"I'm a good guy. You can have your family back, even if you don't open it."

"Really?"

"I'll just change your cot into bunk beds. Or, I could have you all killed. Horrified? Did I hurt your feelings? I was willing to groom you, but you thought you were smarter than me, better than me. You think you have a superpower, yet you have no money. You think I have no power, yet I have more money than anyone. Who's the fool? I am the superpower." He extinguishes the cigarette on the doorjamb and drops the butt on the floor.

"Oh, and one more thing." Like an arcade claw game, Mr. Krone lowers his hand into his inside jacket pocket and struggles to pull out a change purse. "You can keep your useless trinket. It's for amateurs." He tosses it on Bill's desk as he exits.

Bill cracks the venetian blinds of his hangar-facing window.

He watches as a black sedan pulls into the hangar.

Favoring his right leg, Mr. Krone crosses the hangar floor while the driver opens a door for him. Bill waits for the car to back out.

"Aaaaaaaahhhhh!!!" he swipes all the items off his desk onto the floor. The lights in his office flicker and pop.

Beep, beep, beep.

"I KNOW!" He unleashes on the microwave. "I HEARD YOU THE FIRST DAMN TIME! I KNOW MY COFFEE'S READY!"

Bill turns around to see Hack and Ash staring from the break room across the hall. Ash smirks with delight. Bill catches his breath, swipes back his hair, and steps into the doorway. His eyes darting back and forth between the two of them, he snaps, "What?!"

"I love what you've done with the floor," Ash quips, "desperation … it's you."

The remaining light in Bill's office goes out, throwing him into darkness.

THIRTEEN

Infinity

"What couldn't wait?"

"Mr. E, the A.C. honeypot … it caught a fly," Hack says, sidestepping the mess as he enters Bill's office.

"I'm in no mood for jargon." Bill grabs his reading glasses. "You mean we have a fly?"

"Yes … someone clicked the virus. Triangulation shows they're right here in town."

Ash glides his hand over his stubbly scalp. Leaning against the wall, his burly K-N-O-W F-E-A-R fingers move from pocket to pocket in search of chewing tobacco.

Hack places the folder open on Bill's desk. "Here,"—he points to the circled radius on the map— "It was from a phone."

"Do you have the number?"

"The payload got interrupted. I'm still working on that. We should have it soon."

"Schedule a recon fleet for tonight. And wake up Ingrid. We're doing another test."

"About that, Mr. E … the asset's behavior has changed."

"Changed?"

"It's easier if I just show you … do you have a moment?"

"I'll be out in a minute."

"Brilliant!" Hack hopscotches over the desk debris. "I'll fix the lights, prepare the Roids, and get Ingrid going."

"Fix the lights?"

"A couple of lights in the break room burnt …" Hack flicks Bill's light switch repeatedly. "We're gonna need more bulbs," Hack answers and steps out.

"It's adorable how that bright Brit calls you Mr. E," Ash quips from just outside the door. "He's like a nerdy corgi playing a spy."

"And you're a Dick playing Men in Black."

"Are we having a temper tantrum because you're not the star seed anymore. Ha!" Ash closes Bill's door and gives him the finger through the door's window.

∘ ∘ ∘

In front of olive-drab storage room lockers similarly stenciled with H4K and 51ASH, Hack opens his locker and trades his utility vest for a lab coat. Past the lockers, he approaches a wall console. An amber laser scans his face. The console releases three robotic chirps. The screen blinks on, and he taps the glass surface.

"Wake up … ready for a night on the town?"

On an adjacent shelf, dark, satiny spheres begin to move. They are neatly arranged, evenly spaced four-across and three-deep, each about the size of a grapefruit.

Hack's designs are inspired partly by origami, and partly by the protective outer shell beetles open when they're ready to use their wings. Rotors unfurl and extend to prepare for flight. Cobalt blue and amber LEDs blink like the eyes on a sinister spider. Lasers flash on and off, illuminating the shelf space. Each emits small chirps, bloops, and bleeps announcing readiness for deployment.

Diagnostics complete, each drone reverses the process, closing back into its original spherical shape and emitting an affirmative *bleep*. Hack double-checks the screen's report of the Recon Roids' upcoming mission.

"Make me proud," he tells them and heads to the hangar to prepare for the test.

Untangling and connecting cables running from the back of his utility van, Hack cobbles together a poem.

"Connecting gadgets makes me lonely.

To my future sweet, I'm sure you're lovely.

Your electric blue eyes jolt me intensely.

How much longer 'til you are with me?"

I am Infinity.

Hack drops his cables. "Who said that?"

A friend.

"Where are you?" He snatches a flashlight off his workbench and shines it under the van.

You're not alone.

He spins around. "You're in my head!"

Over here.

He tiptoes to the asset in the center of the hangar.

Resembling a giant change purse, the asset is a clamshell gray, roughly ten feet end-to-end. Not perfectly smooth, its surface is dimpled like an orange.

"You're telepathing. Brilliant!"

He runs his hand along the surface the way he would while admiring the finish of a vintage car. He gives it a soft rap. "Hello? Is anybody in there?"

Hello, Hack.

He jumps back. Like breath on a window, the asset's color ripples to a soft pink rose.

He slaps his hands over his mouth to contain his glee and spins around to see if anyone else is there.

Like testing a hot stove, he extends a finger to Infinity's surface. It's cool to the touch. The way one might rouse a napping toddler, he gingerly places a hand on its surface. "Infinity, it is wonderful to finally meet you." Infinity vibrates gently, releasing a purr-like sound. He removes his hand. Along its topmost seam, Hack spies a scattering of opalescent, pink nubs. They elongate into anemone-like tubules. Hack raises his hand. A tubule also rises. As he reaches his hand towards a tubule, it reaches back. Hack's smile grows to a giggle as his fingers and the tubule approach.

Suddenly they all snap back into their shell.

"What are you looking at?"

"Oh my God!" Hack jumps in surprise at the sound of Ash's voice. "Oh, thank God." Hack clutches his chest. "You scared the piss out of me."

"What are you doing?"

"She spoke to me!" He points at the asset.

"Jesus, you need a real woman."

"No, the asset … it's a she. Her name is Infinity … watch!" He blows on the surface, and waves of color wash across it. Hack hovers his hand just inches away, and a blush of cobalt blue blossoms under his palm. "I'm not even touching her … look how she welcomes me." Hack lowers his hand onto the asset.

Ash watches tiny, dewdrop tendrils cling to Hack's hand. "Brilliant! Her metal surface has capillary action," Hack says. Multicolored ripples slowly pulse away from his hand and back again. He peels his palm away. "You try."

"You kidding? I'm not touching that. That's either a Martian pod or a planet killer."

"Come on, Mr. No Fear!"

Ash steps forward. Tentatively he hovers a hand over it. A dark stain spreads across the surface under his hand. Like goosebumps, the stain grows knobby.

"What the hell?" Suddenly Ash's hand is pulled downwards. Bolts of black pulse from his hand across the surface. The entire object loses its color.

"It's got me! Get it off me! Get it off!" As the surface rises around his hand, the tubules emerge again around the topmost seam, this time rapidly. Like a cobra, a tubule rears up and strikes the back of his hand.

"Ow!" He jerks himself free. "It stung me!" Ash inspects the growing welt on the back of his hand as the tubules recede into the asset.

"What the hell's going on?" Bill says, emerging from his office. "Quit fooling around. We've got work to do."

"That thing stung me." Ash shows Bill the welt, already larger than a moment before.

"She slapped an unwelcome hand," Hack offers.

"She?" Bill asks.

"I finally made contact. No … *she* made contact. She spoke to me. Her name is Infinity. Look, I know this sounds crazy. Just … just touch her. See for yourself."

"I wouldn't do that," Ash warns.

"I know you love your gadgets, but *she?*" Bill asks. "This is still a machine … right?"

"I thought so too … but for some reason, she's waking up … it's like she's coming out of hibernation."

"You really think it's female?"

"She showed Ash restraint … like a mother with her petulant child. She could have done far worse."

They both look at Ash.

"Bitch," he says.

"Knuckle dragger. I think Infinity knew exactly who you were, and that is why you got … I believe the term is *bitch slapped."*

"It would be easy to strangle your scrawny little neck with your wires."

"Alright children, we're on the clock," Bill pushes up his sleeves.

"You might need this." Ash pulls a handgun out from the back of his pants. "If she tries to smack you, shoot her." He places the gun on Hack's workbench next to a net-like skullcap full of crisscrossing wires and sensors.

Ash climbs into the back of a box truck from which a cluster of wires trails out from it like colorful spaghetti. The wires travel ten feet from Infinity across the oil-stained, concrete-slab floor and connect to the skullcap on the table.

"Mr. E … what if we change our approach this time?"

"How?"

"Infinity is obviously female. Let's approach her like you want to take her out on a date. How did you entice your wife to date you, open up to you?"

"Excuse me?"

"Think about it. She is sentient. Wooing her might open her up, literally. And ditch the gun; you would never take a gun on a date. You wouldn't make it past a woman's threshold."

"If I get it open …"

"*Her.* If you get *her* to open."

"If I get *her* to open, who knows what might come out. Better safe than sorry."

"Mr. E, give Infinity a chance."

"You're naming it?"

"No, she told me. She spoke to me."

"She spoke to you?"

"Yes … yes she did. I'm telling you—in perfect English I might add—when I went over to her … these tentacle-like *things* sprouted from the top and moved around. Ash saw them too."

Ash flashes his swollen hand at Bill.

"I think she likes me," Hack says proudly.

"Don't make it personal!" Ash hollers.

"Mr. E, this could be the breakthrough we've been looking for. Speak to her … be gentle with her."

"Okay, we'll try it your way."

"Brilliant!" Hack removes the gun from the table.

"It's worth a shot."

"Very punny," Hack says, slipping the gun into a lab-coat pocket.

"Hack?"

"Yes, sir?"

"Leave the gun."

Like a high-tech hairnet, Bill slips the skullcap onto his head. He moves the chair so he can sit facing the object and still see Ash past it in the truck. As he rolls up his sleeves and unbuttons the top of his shirt, Hack peels the backing off adhesive electrode pads, applies them firmly to Bill's chest and forearms, and plugs them into the main cluster of wires.

"Let's see how much of a ladies' man you are," Hack says.

"Sure, no pressure—some of my best work has been with a gun to my head," Bill mutters.

"Beg your pardon, sir?"

"Just go."

Hack joins Ash in the back of the truck. "Ingrid, wake up," Hack commands. The dark bank of monitors inside the truck flash on, washing the interior in a sea of blue-green photons. The software loading screen displays in.grid.

"Audio on." Hack points to Bill, and Bill puts on his headset. "Mr. E, can you hear me?"

Bill gives him a thumbs up.

"Checking your vitals."

"It's been a long time since I went on a blind date," Bill responds through the headset.

"Can you slide the face cam forward a smidge? I'm seeing forehead."

Bill adjusts the skullcap and pouts into the camera mounted on a little pole above his face.

"Much better. Mr. E, according to Ingrid your pout is registering as resentment."

Bill gives the camera a smile.

"Happiness! There you go. I think you missed your calling. You could be an actor. Everyone ready?" He tips prayer hands to Bill, to Ash, and to Infinity. "It's showtime."

Hack takes a few deep breaths and taps a brass Tibetan singing bowl with a wooden mallet. The harmonic *gonngg* reverberates out of the truck and through the hangar, passing the array of crisscrossing, steel support girders, and echoing off the arched ceiling. A sparrow in the metal canopy replies with a cavernous chirp. The impersonal electric hum of the fluorescent lighting fixtures adds to the eerie chorus.

"Mr. E, can you hear the dual-tone?"

Bill gives another thumbs up.

"Then we're cleared for takeoff. Ingrid," Hack says, "start recording. Hmm, your heart rate is elevated … maybe we should postpone?"

"No, let's go!" Bill says, forcing a smile. He returns his attention to the asset, closes his eyes, relaxes his face, and slows and deepens his breath.

"Biofeedback's improving; well done … hemispheres are synchronizing," Hack reports.

"Break it down for me, Sherlock," Ash says. "What are we looking for?"

"We want all those brainwaves to play nice together. You see Infinity's shape … how she's narrowed at the ends and gradually bulges in the middle? This might be a coincidence, but when Mr. E gets into the zone, the shape of his brainwaves on this chart matches her shape."

"We're waiting for him to get into the zone?"

"Here's a fun fact for you: when your theta waves pass a threshold, you click out."

"Click out?"

"Lose consciousness. But by click out, I mean click out of the grid …"

Ash stares back blankly.

"The grid"—Hack waves his hand in the air—"four-dimensional spacetime. Click out, and you can go anywhere in the universe."

"Bullshit."

"Mind your manners, she's listening … unless you want a proper spanking?"

Bloop, bloop, bloop, bloop. The low sonic pulses fill the hangar, one after another, each seemingly coming from a different spot. The object's surface starts to shimmer. A wave of tangerine flashes across it, followed by a sandy yellow. Like veins on a leaf, darker striations come and go. Bumps appear, grow, and disappear. The color changes again, like a passing shadow, now matching the gray of Bill's pants below, the blue of his shirt above, and a crisscross pattern on top.

"That's a good sign." Hack turns back to his displays. "Check it out," he points at a monitor. "See? Bill's brainwaves chart is starting to look like Infinity."

Ash nudges Hack's shoulder and points to the asset. They watch as its skin flinches rough. Then, like soft-serve ice cream on a hot summer day, the whole thing softens.

Hack double-checks the monitors, and his eyes widen.

"Infinity's wavelengths growing, growing … 20,000, 30,000, 40,000 kilometers!"

"What's the big deal?" Ash asks.

"A wavelength of that magnitude can pass straight through the planet, no obstacles."

° ° °

Bill lets his mental clutter fall away.

Inhale.

Exhale.

Mary.

"I have to tell you something," Bill swishes his glass of wine as the two sit close on her couch.

Mary perks up, "Oh?"

"I've had so much fun with you these past few weeks …."

Bill's ears grow hotter the more he speaks. Bill glances at Mary. She slides a lock of her soft brown ringlets of hair back, exposing her ear and its dangly silver earring; he bought her those last week! Simple and straight, the earrings remind him of a magical flute with a rainbow of gems sprinkled along either side. When he gave them to her, she said they were the colors of the seven chakras.

"Yes, me too …" She puts her wine glass down by the candles on the coffee table. He follows her lead; the glass's base lands awkwardly on the coffee table from his shaking hands.

"You're my best friend," he says.

"I feel the same way …."

Bill takes a deep breath. "I'd like us to be more than just friends."

Mary places her hand on his. "Me too."

They move closer on the couch. Bill puts his arms around her, closes his eyes, and kisses her.

Hello, Bill. It's nice to meet you.

Like an octopus changing its colors, a blush of pale peony pink washes over the object, then a sprinkling of iridescent blue rings.

"Mr. E," Bill hears Hack in his headset. "Whatever you did, it's working. I'd like you to vocalize your thoughts though, so I can track and offer guidance."

"You're looking beautiful today …," Bill says.

"Call her Infinity."

"… Infinity. Will you open for me?"

"Too soon," Hack says. "Woo her more."

"Throw me a line. I'm a little lost here."

"Remember dating? Ask her about her."

Bill slides his hands along his thighs. "So … Infinity, where are you from?"

Everywhere.

"Do you have any interests?"

You.

"Me?"

Another rainbow shimmer washes over the object. Hack pushes Mute, cutting off Bill's audio feed. "Ash look at this, he's blushing. Oh, my goodness. Infinity's wave is acknowledging that he's blushing, and she's blushing back." Infinity flashes crimson.

Bill shifts in his seat. "Are you alive?"

Are you alive?

"Are you self-aware?"

Are you self-aware?

"I recognize myself when I look in the mirror."

Is what you see in the mirror you?

"Now you're starting to sound like Mira."

I'm Infinity.

"Can you open for me?"

I am open. Can you open for me?

"No, you're not open. You're still the same."

No, you're not open. You're still the same.

"Now, stop that." Bill jumps up, knocking over his chair. Hack quickly restores Bill's audio feed. "Mr. E, your stress levels are going up," he whispers into Bill's headset.

"This is not gonna end well," Ash says.

"Will you open for me?"

Will you open for me?

"Jesus," Bill mutters. "Hack, we need another approach. This is not working."

"I don't understand, she was delightful to me."

Bill glances at the venetian blinds. Mr. Krone's image flashes in his head.

You're a fraud … you'd be less pathetic if you admitted it.

"What just happened?" Hack scans the myriad of readouts.

"His anxiety is spiking. Mr. E, I'd like you to return to your seat. Mr. E …"

You've got until the end of the week.

The object dims and turns the color of oil-stained concrete.

"Mr. E, what's happened?" Hack asks. "You're losing contact."

The object becomes black again.

"It just got personal," Ash adds with a smirk.

"Oh no, we're back to baseline … we lost it. Uh, oh,"—Hack points at the monitor—"here comes rage …"

Red-faced, Bill rips off his headgear, grabs the pistol from the table, and steps towards Infinity. His adhesive pads tug at him. He rips them off to free himself. "I'm asking nicely. Open."

"Your buddy's about to go off the deep end," Ash says, smiling.

Bill raises the gun. "OPEN!" he barks. Infinity turns gunmetal gray.

"Mr. E! Don't!"

"Don't shoot the cars!" Ash yells.

Bill lets out a guttural yell, aims away from the object, and fires repeatedly around the hangar. Hack and Ash dive to the floor of the box truck. Bullets strike the windowless vans, SUVs, and a candy-apple red sports car.

The pling, pling, plings of bullets striking metal is followed by a new sound. A loud, electronic, animalistic, wounded 'Mhmmf' engulfs the hangar.

Silence.

Ash scrambles to his feet; Bill is aiming the gun at Infinity.

"I *need* you to OPEN," Bill demands.

"You've got one bullet left," Ash says. "Make it count! Shoot her!"

"Don't shoot her!" Hack screams, jumping out of the truck.

"Stay away!" Bill aims the gun at Hack, and Hack dives for

cover under the truck.

"OPEN!" Bill fires at Infinity.

Whimpt!

"Ow!" Bill yelps.

Ash jumps out of the truck, snatches the gun, and shoves Bill to the floor. He rushes to the sports car.

"GODDAMMIT! You shot Janie's car!"

"Ingrid, stop recording!" Hack yells from underneath the truck. He pulls himself out, grabs the first-aid kit, and hurries to Bill.

Bill sits up. Blood emerges from the gash on his shoe.

"DAMMIT!"

"Not a good first date, Mr. E."

Ash runs his finger over the bullet hole in the rear bumper of the sports car. "Janie's gonna kill me."

FOURTEEN

You Are Now Leaving Your Senses

There's always another way.

Grimacing, Bill slips off his shoe, then peels away his blood-soaked sock. He grabs the rubbing alcohol from the first-aid kit. Gritting his teeth, he opens the bottle and lets its contents trickle onto the three-inch gash running across the top of his left foot. He pours more onto cotton balls and dabs them on the bullet wound.

I heal rapidly.

He hops to the paper towels and rips one off. He sits back down, pats the wound dry, and locates the biggest bandage from the kit.

Oh, who am I kidding? He pushes his ring out of the way to scratch his finger. _My thoughts don't matter._

He carefully applies the bandage, grabs the bloody sock, and pulls it back over his foot.

"Hack?" Bill hollers.

"Yes?" Hack pokes his head into the room. "Are you alright?"

"Are the Roids set for tonight?"

"Yes, we'll have positive ID by morning."

"Good."

"Sir?"

Bill looks up at Hack.

"What was she like?"

Bill reaches under his desk and pulls out a pair of sneakers.

"Infinity? It kept repeating back whatever I said. It was juvenile."

"Repeating?—Fascinating."

"Fascinating? She sounded like a broken record."

"It would be unreasonable to assume that a foreign entity's mode of communication would instantly make sense to us. I wouldn't be that surprised if an alien species' way of communicating seemed absurd by our standards."

"Occam's Razor," Bill volleys back. "Infinity was parroting me like a brat. Her programing's corrupted. That's the simplest explanation."

"Was she parroting you," Hack asks, "or was she parenting you?"

"Parenting?"

"I ran across similar communication divides while getting my doctorate in anthropology. Think about it … if Infinity is a more advanced species, and if she were benevolent …"

"That's two big ifs."

"I know, but hear me out … if she is advanced and

benevolent, throwing your questions back at you can be a meaningful form of communication. You asked her if she was self-aware. I'm guessing she asked you the same question, which is why you said you recognize yourself in the mirror." Bill carefully slips a sneaker onto his bandaged foot.

"That's one definition of self-awareness," Hack says. "Another is awareness of how you're feeling in any given moment and *why*. When we are oblivious to why we feel what we feel—or even what we feel at all—we may even lose control of faculties, and I don't know … empty a weapon indiscriminately in a fit of rage."

"Are you lecturing me?"

"Is she trying to show us what we look like to her? From her point of view, are we just heavily armed apes?"

Ash appears in the doorway.

"Exhibit A," Hack announces.

"I'm taking Janie's car to the dealer; I'll bring you the bill," he points a finger at Bill, turns on his heels, and disappears from the doorway.

"I think we should give Infinity more credit. I tip my cap to any woman who demonstrates the perfect amount of restraint with that Neanderthal."

Bill pulls his laces tight. "Okay."

"Shall we try again?"

"Not now."

"I think you're right. I'll log this pause due to *personal inclemency*."

Bill runs his fingers through his hair.

"Anything else I can help with?"

"Thanks," Bill's eyes are red from fighting back tears, "no."

"Very good," Hack says as he gently closes the door.

Bill closes his eyes, but someone's voice breaks the silence.

A gun?

Mira is sitting across from him.

"Mira, I need your help. I need to open this or …"

Wake up, she says and vanishes.

"*Dammit,* Mira."

Mira … Mirage. Bill busts out laughing. Stretching as far back as his chair will go and gazing past the ceiling, he says, "I'm not listening to you. You're a mirage."

He straightens himself and sifts through the honeypot folder.

Who clicked the link? Joe? Unlikely. Who else would be so curious as to click?

Jerry? They'll rip him to shreds. How can I contact him first and without Mr. Krone finding out? Think … think!

Ha! That's it … "think!" Bill closes his eyes to concentrate.

Jerry, go to Longbranch.

. . .

Jerry tugs at the bottom of his Phish T-shirt. His profuse stomach keeps peeking out. It's the same one he wore the last time he spoke with Bill at the Longbranch, but a decade ago, it fit better. Rounding the corner, his heart jumps at the sight of their old meeting place down the street.

He regrets how he handled himself the last time they met.

After all, he and Bill were best friends, true brothers. They saw eye to eye on most things. Their mutual trust allowed them to speak candidly and joyfully.

Their last conversation at the diner began simply enough, over a cup of coffee.

"Mr. Krone made me an offer," Bill says.

"Dude, are you kidding? No. The answer is no. Don't even consider it."

"I know. I'm gonna turn it down."

"The fact that you even talked to him at all … he's bad news."

"I've got a handle on it. Don't worry."

"I don't think you've got a handle on it. You're dealing with some scary stuff."

"Jerry …"

"I love you man, but it's time for me to walk away. And you should too. Get out before you're sucked into their war."

"Jerry …"

"I have a family I have to think about. You should think about your family, too."

The jingle of the doorbell as Jerry enters the diner brings him back to the present moment. He sits at the same booth where they had their last conversation, and a waitress brings him a menu and silverware wrapped in a napkin. He grabs his prescription aviator-style glasses from his T-shirt's collar and pretends to study the menu.

Jerry?

"Bill?"

Heyyyy, you can hear me?

"Yeah. I haven't done this in a long time. I thought I lost the ability until I heard you call out to me the other day."

I missed you.

Ditto, brother. You were MIA.

I was.

It's been what … more than ten years? I thought you never wanted to speak to me again.

I thought the same thing. I waited for you to reach out.

So we both waited. I had stopped … cold turkey.

Why?

Mira told me what happened to you. I have a family, so I had to stop.

Why stop everything?

You know. People look at you like you've got two heads."

"Are you ready to order?" The waitress says.

Jerry strokes his scraggly beard, now more salt than pepper; it matches his hair. "Cold turkey sandwich," he says, drawing it out. "And water is fine … thanks, sweetheart."

"I'll put that right in for you," the waitress says, taking his menu.

It's good to know that we can still talk.

I haven't seen you in over ten years. When I heard your voice, I had to come."

Why stop everything?

It's terrifying. Everybody who experiences what we have … everybody either goes loony or stops. Those are your only choices.

Ignorance is comfortable. Jerry rips the paper off one end of his straw and blows it straight up, catching the attention of a little girl sitting with her mother at an adjacent table.

You're capable of so much more. We all are.

"There are some things man shouldn't touch."

You said that out loud.

Jerry looks around. The little girl nudges her mother. "Don't stare. Mind your business, and eat your grilled cheese," the mother says.

How does that happen, Bill? Jerry looks down, pretending to play with his phone.

I don't know how it happens ... all I know is it happens. Mira was too intense for me. It's like she could part your flesh, stare straight into your soul, and show you all your flaws. I don't want to look at my flaws every day. You know what I mean? It was too much,—he shakes his head—*It was too much.*

The waitress returns with his water, "Your food will be right out."

Have you seen us online?

Have you been listening to me? I'm out. I don't go looking for trouble.

What about Mary?

Sorry ... lost touch.

Where is Mira?

Jerry takes his time unrolling the napkin and placing his utensils. He whispers, "Like I told you, we all split up. No contact. Bill, I'm glad to have you back, but don't suck me back into that world … it's all in the past."

Hush.

Let's be grateful for what we've got. And get yourself back home where you belong. I wish you were here with me.

Jerry looks at the seat across from him. "Dude! You're bilocating!"

Impossible.

"What happened to your face?"

Impossible.

With that, Bill's image vanishes.

Jerry jumps when the waitress places a second glass of water in front of him.

"Will your friend be wanting coffee when he gets back?"

"It's just me."

"I saw a guy sitting across from you."

"Sorry … just me." Jerry smiles and shrugs.

She removes her glasses and inspects them with a squint.

"Now I'm seeing ghosts."

She saw you … the waitress.

I don't believe you.

Man … that's why you're stuck. You don't believe. Jerry busts out laughing. "She saw you!" He leans back, looks around, and pulls at his hair. Grinning ear to ear, he cheers to the girl, "She saw him!" She shrinks back towards her mom. He slaps the table. "She saw him." Jerry removes his glasses to wipe away the tears.

The mother takes her daughter's hand and gets up quickly to

pay at the front register.

Jerry notices a plush kitty forgotten on their bench. "Excuse me." He waves the kitty at them. The mother nods, and the girl runs to him, sneakers blinking with every step.

"Kiki!" She takes her toy and looks at Jerry excitedly. She cups her fingers around her mouth, and Jerry leans in. "I saw the ghost, too," she whispers.

∘　∘　∘

A gun?

"Mira,"—Bill says, opening a can of tomato soup with red pepper—"Mr. Krone's given me until the end of the week or he's going to kill me and my family. I need your help opening Infinity. If I have to toast it like a marshmallow with a flamethrower to open it and save my family that's what I'll do." He pours the soup into a fine china bowl. As he steps barefoot across the marble floor to the microwave, he looks down and makes a mental note to change the blood-stained bandage soon. He pops the bowl into the microwave.

There's always another way.

"Then tell me. You and your navel-gazing got me into this mess ... now help me out. I need to live in the real world."

The blame game is like solitaire ... you're playing against yourself. When your mind is free, you are free.

"Enough nonsense! They're going after my family now." A glint of purple from the sapphire in his ring catches his eye. "My *powers*—if I even have any— aren't helping. It's time for me to return to reality."

What did you learn in the hole?

"I'm still in the hole."

You're not open to listening.

"Open? I've been open to listening to you for what, a dozen years? What's it gotten me? I've lost my family. I've been driven to the brink of madness—if I'm not already there— and now I've got less than a week to open this or we're all dead."

You're traumatized.

He scratches at his ring finger. "I'm delusional. I'm having a conversation with the voices in my head! I imagined I talked to Jerry … I could swear I was right there with him. *Jesus.* I even believed that you visited me while I was in the hole. That's trauma! Utter delusion."

Let's talk tomorrow.

"Tomorrow's not gonna change anything. I've done it your way. I need to do things my way from now on."

Bill pulls Mr. Krone's change purse out of his pocket. He pulls out a lone piece of paper. Written on it, in Mr. Krone's handwriting and underlined three times, Bill reads:

My children respect me.

He dumps the note in his waste bin, grabs a pen and a stickie note off his counter, and writes: *I get my family back.*

Bill stuffs the note in the change purse and the microwave dings. Bill opens the door and grabs the bowl of soup with both hands. He lifts it, but the bowl is too hot. It topples out of the microwave, crashes to the marble floor, and explodes, sending soup and shards of fine china everywhere.

Bill stares at the destruction and disarray at his feet. Soup splattered and dripping on his white cabinets like a fresh crime scene, his face contorts into a grimace.

"Aaaaaaaah!!!" The kitchen lights flicker.

He lowers himself—placing his hands and knees into the soup—and surveys the miniature landscape of destruction around him. Like a child finger painting, he uses his right index to create a picture in the soup. The drawing begins to take shape. Like an eye, his Infinity drawing stares back at him.

"Mary … WJ … I'm sorry."

Finding the largest part of the bowl, the base, and half a side, he slides it close to him. He locates another big piece. Like a puzzle, he sets it back on the base. He plucks another shard from the mess and gingerly sets it on the bowl, but the first piece falls out.

He rests his back against the counter drawers and splays his legs out in front of him. Looking like a wounded warrior, he pushes the broken bowl away and slumps lower.

"Mary …"

He looks at his hands, drenched in tomato soup like those of a murderer, and sobs.

o o o

A Recon Roid flies, dark and silent, following the gently scalloped path of power lines as they sag from pole to pole. The Roid pauses and hovers outside the illumination of a nearby streetlight.

When it resumes its flight, it ducks behind the far side of a house, eventually reappearing around back, pausing at each window. It drifts towards the next house, stopping inches away from an upstairs window. Flying with the grace and silence of an owl, the room on the other side is undisturbed. Inside, a phone blinks on. An LED on the Roid lights up, transforming the dark room into a uniform hue of ultramarine blue. The light strobes slowly then accelerates its tempo and blinks off. Next, an amber laser light scans the room from right to left, eventually finding someone asleep in their bed. The Roid turns to inspect and identify. The occupant mutters and shifts under the blanket. The scanner ceases. The drone departs, returning the room to darkness. The phone goes back to sleep. Lily rolls over.

I Remember This Place

"No, no, no! He's just a child! Please God, help me!"

As his mother holds him tight against his chest, WJ buries his face into her bosom.

"Leave them!"

The muffled voice is unfamiliar.

"Thank you, thank you," Mary sobs.

WJ lifts his head at the sound of an arriving police cruiser. He catches a glimpse of the heron flying away. The storm has retreated; far off, creamsicle-tinged clouds frame a robin's-egg-blue sky.

Wake up.

Bwoop! Will rubs the sleep out of his eyes so he can see his phone.

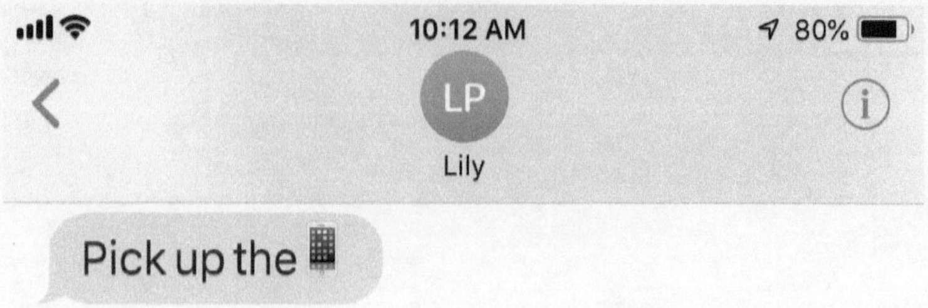

Will smiles at Lily's text. When the phone rings, he eagerly answers. "Hey, Lily!"

"Hey, Will! Do you want to go to the park and hike the hill?"

"Sure."

"I'll meet you there at eleven!"

"Okay … sounds like fun. See you there." Will hangs up and checks the time. "Crap!" He leaps out of bed, scans his bedroom floor for any usable clothing, grabs a shirt, and sniffs its pits. He wrinkles his nose, drops the shirt like a rancid potato, sniffs his armpit, and recoils from the smell.

A quick shower later, he finds a lively striped T-shirt to go with his blue jeans and his favorite red-and-blue windbreaker. "Phew," he mutters at the clock on his phone, "still time for breakfast," and zips down the stairs.

Crunching through a bowl of cereal, he wonders what the day will bring. He slurps the remaining milk from the bowl and bounds back up the stairs two at a time. He locates his backpack, dumps its contents on the floor, and the change purse tumbles out. He grabs a notepad, tears off a piece from a sheet, and writes:

Lily and I are together

He folds it up, sticks it in the change purse, and tosses the change purse in his backpack. "Do I need a backpack?" he asks himself. "Oh!" He brings it downstairs to the kitchen and scoots around his mom to grab two water bottles, fill them, and add them to his inventory.

"*Two* water bottles?"

"I'm meeting Lily at the park."

"Oh, that's thoughtful of you. Bring snacks too."

"Mom, I'm going to be late!"

"Then think fast." She tosses two packages of trail mix at him. Will catches them in his opened backpack, zips it, throws his backpack over a shoulder, and rushes out the door.

"Have …"

The door slams shut with a ka-chunk.

"… fun!"

o   o   o

Out of breath from biking at top speed, Will's heart jumps at the sight of Lily at the park entrance, arms crossed, tapping a foot, a dour look on her face.

"I'm late. I'm so sorry." As he fumbles with his bike lock, Will looks up at Lily. Her grim expression turns to mischievous glee.

"Race you!" she blurts out and starts sprinting to the forested hill across the park.

"What? Hey!" Will stumbles around the bike rack to catch up. He sprints past ornamental cherry trees in full bloom, dusting the surrounding grass with pink and white petals. *I'll appreciate them on the way back.*

The trailhead is not far off, but Lily is fast. Despite his handicap, he's catching up. Will slows his gait.

"I win!" Lily thrusts her fists in the air. Between huffs and puffs and hands on knees, they both giggle with glee. Lily's childlike lightness and natural ebullience are intoxicating and contagious.

As they set out on the trail, Will and Lily step to the side to accommodate a couple coming down the trail with their yellow lab.

"Hello," Lily says with a wave. "See any cool birds?"

"We saw a cardinal," the woman replies.

"Nice hiking boots," Lily adds.

"Thanks! I know. Totally overkill for this molehill, but they're brand new, and I wanted to break them in. Enjoy!"

"Thanks!" Lily rubs the dog's head as he passes.

"Who was that?" Will asks.

"I dunno … some hikers."

"Oh, the way you talked, I thought you knew them."

"Nope. Nice dog, though."

As they continue, Will feels the sun intermittently warming his back as they pass from shadow to sunlight. He drops his head back to look at the natural cathedral of tall trees, the new foliage a luminous display of greens.

Will scans the path ahead. The mossy, damp rock outcroppings look like little excerpts from a pastoral painting. The sound of traffic fades as they make their way up the path.

In this patch of forest on this tiny hill, what Will notices most of all is Lily: her beatific smile, her short, utilitarian ponytail, her sea-foam green Hampton Beach hoodie with navy blue lettering, her faded jeans, and white sneakers. She'd make an Abercrombie and Fitch model wilt. There was something comforting about her that made him feel alive with confidence.

"Oh … listen!" She stops. "Hear that high-pitched whining Peeeeeep. Peeeeeep?"

"Yeah."

"Cedar waxwings! Here …" She grabs her backpack and pulls out a well-worn bird book. "My grandpa taught me all about birding. This was his book." She finds the page for cedar waxwings. "See? They're beige, but they have a black mask on their face."

"Oh! There it is!" He points in the direction of the sound.

"There are all these birds all around us," she says. "If you memorized their calls, you could identify them with your eyes closed." She returns the bird book to her backpack.

Will squints into the sky. He can make out a hawk circling upwards on a warm updraft.

He reaches around and grabs a bottle from the side-netting on his backpack. "Water?"

"Oh, thanks!" She grabs the bottle, takes a drink, and starts back up the trail, making sure to walk beside him. "What do you dream about?"

"Like *dream* dreams?"

"Yeah."

"I have these secret-agent-slash-superhero dreams."

"With a cape and a mask and everything?" Lily chuckles.

"I never look at my body. But if I had to guess, more secret agent than superhero. Remember the time Joe told us to name our negative voices?"

"Yeah?"

"I had a dream that night We were running in a field …"

"We? As in you and me?" Lily rocks towards him.

"Um, yeah," Will blushes. "I was on a mission, and you were with me, and someone was chasing us through a field. I wanted to confront him, so I told you to run to a gazebo. When I saw his face, it was me!"

"Oh … was it Oscar?" She nibbles at her pinkie nail.

"Yeah, that's what I thought. But it gets weirder. He said *I* was Oscar. He told me to wake up; he pushed me off a cliff, and I fell out of bed."

Water sprays from Lily's mouth. "I'm sorry … I shouldn't be laughing."

"It's okay. Now that I think about it, it's kind of funny. But it wasn't at the time. Your turn. What about you? What do you dream about?"

"I have this recurring dream where I own a big house, and it needs a lot of work. My husband and I are fixing it up: the floors, the wallpaper, the furniture."

"That sounds nice. And it sounds like you know what you want when you grow up."

"Well, I'm no superhero."

"I think you're pretty super." *Did I say that out loud? Idiot!* Lily smiles and lifts a tendril of hair off the side of her face. As they approach the top, the view opens onto the surrounding area. They head to an outcropping of lichen-covered boulders with a view of the park below. A gazebo abuts an adjacent field.

Lily finds a flat rock and sits, leaving room for Will.

"I love your mom and her explanation about names. Mr. Boooorrrhr," Lily chuckles.

"Lily Powers." Will adds with an awkward chuckle. "Lilies don't have powers. Wait, that didn't come out right. Lilies are great, they're so … *pretty*."

"Lilies have powers. Lilies take dirt—which is basically worm *crap*, you know—and from crap they create life, but not just life … also *oxygen* for you and me and everyone else that can't make their own. If that wasn't enough, they manage to be *pretty* while doing all of that. Now that's badass."

After a moment of silence, she bumps shoulders with Will and then turns to face him. They fall silent, staring directly into each other's eyes. Lily brushes the hair from her face. Her hair's colors layer from shimmering brown to light blonde. Will closes his eyes, and they both lean in. As their lips touch, his dream flashes in his mind: *"Come on! He's coming!" He makes out the outline of a gazebo in the distance. "There! Run! Go! Go! Go!"*

Will abruptly pulls away and scans the area.

Lily opens her eyes. "Will?"

His eyes are drawn to the field and the gazebo. "We gotta go."

"Wait … what?"

"I remember this place. We need to leave,"—he scrambles to his feet—"… NOW!"

They grab their things and race down the hill.

"I don't understand," she asks without slowing down.

"What's going on?"

"This is gonna sound crazy. This is where my dream was."

"Dream?"

"The Oscar dream … the field, the gazebo, it all matches. …"

They don't stop until they reach their bikes. While she unlocks hers, Lily catches her breath and looks around nervously.

"Something's coming," Will says. "I can feel it. We need to leave here fast." He hops on his bike. As they head out of the park, Will makes sure to move fast but not leave Lily in his wake. He glances back to see if anyone is following them. Facing forward, he swerves as a mother yanks her stroller back from the street just in time to miss being hit.

"Sorry!" he yells as he passes her.

"I'm sorry," Will tells Lily. "This is crazy."

Lily glances at him, her face a mix of fear and determination.

"I trust you, Will. Turn!"

They lean into the intersection as they turn.

Lily slows her pace as they approach her neighborhood. "I can make it home from here."

"You sure?"

"Yeah, text me when you're home," she says and veers away.

As the two peel off in opposite directions, Will looks over his shoulder and catches the sight of her backpack bouncing on her back.

o   o   o

Nearing home, Lily passes a black SUV with police lights parked on the side of the street, the NO FEAR bumper sticker catches her eye.

She glances over her shoulder as the vehicle pulls into the street behind her. She slows, coasting as close to the curb as she can to let it by, but it stays behind her, matching her pace.

The hair on the back of her neck stands up when she rounds the corner onto her street, and the SUV follows her. She picks up her pace as the vehicle nears her back tire.

Her foot wobbles and slips off a peddle. "Come on, almost home," she mutters.

Bwoop! The lights on top of the vehicle flash. Then it speeds up, swerves, and stops abruptly, cutting her off. The passenger-side door flies open. Ash steps out and adjusts his sunglasses.

"Be nice," Hack calls out from behind the wheel.

Ash tugs at his cuffs as he comes around the front of the vehicle. Standing broad and tall, he lowers his face into hers. "Lily Powers?"

o   o   o

You're making me nervous, CALL ME, Will texts.

"What do you think ... chicken or pasta?" Mom asks as she makes her way from the couch to the kitchen. "That's some fog out there,"—she says, peeking out the kitchen window—"you're in for the night." She leans closer to the window. "Will ... the police are here; that's strange."

Will joins his mother at the window. His stomach sinks.

Lily.

They watch the policemen as they pass under their kitchen window and go to their side door.

Will pulls her hand away from the doorknob. "Mom, don't open the door. They may not be real police."

"WJ, what are you talking about? They just got out of the car. That's a real police car parked in our driveway."

Like an animal clawing its way out of his chest, Will's heart pounds fiercely. A pain twists his stomach into a knot.

Mary opens the door. Two police officers stand in the doorway, an older man and his younger counterpart.

Will's face flushes hot. He feels exposed, standing in the middle of his kitchen. Jittery, he stares at the officers but isn't able to take them in. He remembers this feeling. It was how he felt in his dreams when he had to fight. Something is wrong. Horribly wrong. He has to trust his instincts and not the two men who look like policemen. They could be A.U. He needs a weapon. His eyes lock on the butcher block knife holder in the corner of the kitchen counter, and he takes a step back.

"Mrs. Freeman?"

"Yes?"

"Sorry to bother you this evening, I'm Officer McGeough. We understand your son was with Lily Powers today?" Will's face goes pale.

"Yes, they went to the park this morning." Mary glances back at Will. "Why? Is anything wrong?"

"When did you last see her?" The older officer asks Will.

"We went to the park. Then we biked together to her neighborhood." Will hears the words come out of his mouth. "We weren't far from her house when I left her. What happened?" His knees go weak.

"What time?"

"I'm not sure. One, one fifteen. I got home around … early afternoon maybe?"

"1:30. You came in around 1:30," Mary quickly confirms.

"Lily didn't make it home today. You were the last person to see her. Any information you give us could be crucial."

"She was wearing white sneakers, jeans, and a Hampton Beach hoodie. She had a gray backpack … with pink piping. And she had pink nail polish, but her pinkie nail is chipped; she bites it."

"We found her backpack on the side of the road."

"Did it have a bird book in it?"

"Yes, is that significant?"

"Her grandfather gave it to her. She'd never leave it on purpose. Somebody took her!"

"Took her? Do you know who?"

"I … no," Will shakes his head. "I don't. But Rich Fartman … Artman's house has security cameras on the front door. Check their cameras. His house is before Lily's house. She would have to pass his house on her way to hers."

"We're asking all the neighbors for any cam footage. What's Rich Artman's house number?"

"Twelve. His house is the biggest one on the street." Will scrunches his face. "Perfect landscaping, the tallest flagpole … the one with a white picket fence."

"Officers," Mary says, "please find her."

"We're going to do everything in our power to bring her back quickly and safely."

"Thank you," Mary says and closes the door.

As they pass under the window, officer McGeough presses the button on his shoulder mic. "Issue an amber alert for Lily Powers."

"Oh, WJ, I'm so sorry," his mom gives Will a long hug. "This is horrible."

"Mom …"

"Yeah?"

"I knew something bad was going to happen today. I should've biked with her all the way home."

"Don't blame yourself."

"You don't understand. I knew. I should've brought her all the way home!" Will bolts to his room and collapses onto his bed. His stomach sinks, and nausea sets in.

Who can help …?

His phone rings, an alien avatar flashes on the screen, and he picks up.

"Willis …"

"Russell … Lily's missing!"

"What?"

"Something's happened to her. What do I do?"

"Take a breath, I'm sure she's fine. Track her on your phone."

"Oh … right!" His hands shaking, Will taps on his phone. "It can't find her."

Bwoop! Bwoop!

"Dude. Did an amber alert for Lily pop up on your phone?"

"I told you!"

A fearful Lily flashes in Will's head. Then a giant change purse in an arched hangar.

"I saw it."

"Saw what?"

"Dude, I just had a vision."

"Your first vision, cool!"

"I saw an airplane hangar. She's in an airplane hanger."

"I knew there was something to those dreams you kept having. Willis, you're psychic!"

"No, I'm not."

"Denial is a river in Egypt. You are psychic! I'm not alone anymore. Do you know what this means? It means we're going to be unstoppable, bruh."

"Russell, focus. We've got to find Lily."

"Okay, okay, okay. I know there's one airstrip in town. I'm pulling up a map. Found it. It's called *Aviators Unlimited.* Hang on … that's weird," Russell says. "They don't have a website … or hours … or anything."

"Aviators Unlimited … A.U. shit, she's in danger … and it's all my fault!"

"Slow the truck down. The A.U.?"

"It's a long story."

"I thought you weren't into conspiracy theories."

"I'm not. You've heard of them?"

"Do you even *know* me? Of course, I've heard of them! They control *everything*."

"What do we do? We can't call the cops."

"This is a new side of you."

"We need a car. What about your brother? Can he bring us?"

"I'm on it … be right over."

"*Don't* come to the door. I'll meet you outside."

"I'll be there in five."

"Thanks, Russell."

"Anything for my other brother. We got a *mission!*"

Will quickly tears off a piece of paper, writes: *I save Lily*, stuffs it in the change purse, and crams it into his jeans pocket. He scurries downstairs and halts at the kitchen door. He grabs a dry-erase pen and writes on the whiteboard on the

fridge: *With Russell. Gone to find Lily.*
He heads out the door and slips into the darkness.

PART THREE

ILLUMINATION

SIXTEEN

Reunion

"THE AWAKENING OF the man in the boy and the soul within the body is the emergence of humanity."

—Wen

The headlights of the SUV pulling into the hangar flash on Bill's office wall. Ash gets out of the SUV and does a hard point to its back row. Bill makes out the outline of a body. Blonde hair peeks out from underneath the black hood. As he approaches, Ash opens the door and pulls the hood off Lily, trails of tears blemishing her face. She takes a deep breath of fresh air.

"Out," Ash says, cutting the zip tie restraints and pulling her out of the vehicle by an arm.

"A girl?" Bill asks.

"Mr. E, it was her phone," Hack says.

"Shit." Bill turns to Lily. "Well, where is it?"

"Where's what?" Lily replies, squinting and cowering beside the vehicle.

Bill shows her Mr. Krone's change purse.

"You mean Will's …."

"WJ?" Bill's heart flutters, then sinks.

"Oh my gosh, You're Will's father!"

"You know my son?"

"Better than you."

"Mr. Krone is gonna love this."

"Ash, shut up."

"You're not going to hurt me,"—she wipes her cheeks with her palms— "because you'd never hurt anyone Will cares about."

"I said shut up!" He turns to Hack, "You got her phone?"

Hack pulls it out of a black bag and hands it to Bill.

"Unlock it," Bill says to Lily.

"No."

"Ash," Bill says.

Ash steps towards Lily and sticks a hand inside his suit.

"Okay, okay!" She unlocks her phone and hands it to Bill.

Ash pulls out his tobacco tin.

He finds Will in her contacts and hands the phone back to Hack. "Track him and bring him to me— I don't care what he does to you. Don't you lay a finger on him."

"Sounds like fun."

"I mean it."

"Do I tell you how to do your job?"

"He's my son!"

"Don't get your panties in a bunch. I'll deliver your package, undamaged, right into those baby-soft hands of yours. What do you want me to do with her?" Ash asks.

"Put her in the break room."

∘ ∘ ∘

"Where's John?" Will asks, buckling himself into the passenger seat.

"He's texting some girl," Russell says. "We got this."

"You can't drive."

"How do you think I got here? Stay focused. Now, why would the A.U. want Lily?"

"I think it has something to do with this." Will pulls the change purse out and shows Russell.

Russell turns it over in his hand. "This shape reminds me of something, but I can't put my finger on it."

"It belonged to my dad." Will pulls out his wallet and locates the business card. "Lily and I have been going here."

"Where'd you find this card?"

"From Joe. Lily and I met him at Hannaford's. He has a change purse too. We've been going to his house after school."

Russell's eyebrows go up. "Just when I thought tonight couldn't get any weirder … you know Master Wen?"

"His name is Joe."

"*Joe?* I'm not sure how to tell you this dude, but your guy is an imposter."

"No, he's legit. My mom knows him."

"He's not Master Wen, and I should know. Master Wen is an

enigma in UFOlogy circles. Totally off the grid … and she's a woman. What if this guy is A.U.?"

"I told you, my mom knows him. And my dad knew him, too. We have to go."

"Dude, I'm telling you: Wen is a woman. Hey Iris," Russell tells his phone, "take me to Aviator's Unlimited."

° ° °

"I'm going to have to lock you in here," Hack tells Lily. "There's food if you want," he points to snacks on the break room counter. "And magazines … and a bathroom." Hack motions towards the far end of the room. "The chairs aren't very comfortable," he manages an awkward chuckle, running his hand along the back of an industrial-looking metal chair with a wood seat and back.

Still shaking, she darts her eyes to Hack.

"It's not home but try to make yourself comfortable. Hopefully, this will all be over soon."

"You're going to kill me?"

"Oh no, I didn't mean it that way! What I meant was, well, I think this will all work out."

"Make yourself comfortable?" Ash repositions his chaw with his tongue. "This ain't no resort," he says, pressing his finger into Hack's chest, "and you ain't her butler."

Ash turns to Lily. "You wanna know your odds of getting out of here?" He spits his chewing tobacco onto the floor, spattering it on her white sneakers. "They're the same as me cleaning that up." He turns to Hack, "Let's go."

Lily shakes her foot to flick the brown chaw-sputum sludge off her sneaker. "Gross."

o   o   o

"Yellow light," Will points to the intersection up ahead.

"I got this." Russell presses down on the pedal.

"Yellow light means slow down! The fog is thick … we can barely see."

"We're on a mission." Russell breezes through the red light.

"Dude, you just blew through that red light in front of a cop!"

"Oops, my bad."

The police cruiser stopped crosswise at the intersection peels out in pursuit. A blush of red and blue reflects off the dash.

"Oh no," Will shudders, looking in his side-view mirror.

"What do you mean, oh no? This is great. Now we've got back up!" Russell says.

"No! No cops. Lily could get hurt."

Russell speeds up.

"What are you doing? Pull over."

"Time for evasive maneuvers."

"You're gonna try to outrun a cop in the fog?" Will asks frantically.

"In a quarter mile, your destination will be on the left," Iris reports.

"I got this." Russell grips the wheel tighter and speeds up.

"No, no, no, no, no!"

"I told you, I got this! I crushed it in Forza," Russell

announces as his face flashes red and blue from the police car's lights.

"This isn't a video game!" Will screams over the siren.

The cruiser, lighting up the fog like a futuristic cauldron, suddenly shrinks in their mirrors.

"Where did they go?" Will asks, twisting in his seat.

"They're not gonna chase us in the fog; it's too dangerous. I told you, I got this. Russell slows down and checks his side-view mirror.

"Your destination is ahead on the left."

"Yes! We made it. We're home free."

Flashing red lights fill the car's interior.

"They're back!" Will says.

"Okay! Sprint's over," Russell says as he speeds up.

"You have arrived at your destination."

They speed past a small, unlit sign for Aviators Unlimited.

"Recalculating."

"Shut up, Iris!" Russell barks.

"We can't outrun the police, pull over."

"If you can hear me, this would be a good time to beam us up!"

"Who are you talking to?"

"Aliens. They're all around us. Be quiet, I'm manifesting."

"What the …"

A tall bird, standing on the yellow line in the street, emerges from the fog in front of them. Russell swerves as the bird takes flight; passing directly over them, its wingspan is as wide as their windshield.

"What the heck was that?" Russell says.

"Harry!" Will whips his head around. The police cruiser swerves, screeches to a stop, and fades into the fog along with Harry.

"Way to go, Harry."

"You know that bird?"

"Yeah … yeah, I do."

"Shape-shifting alien?"

"Make a legal u-turn," Iris announces.

"Time to drift!"

"No!" Will yells.

"Hang on!" As their car slices through the fog, Russell turns off the headlights.

"Dude, what are you doing? We can't see!" Will places his hands on the dash to brace himself.

"And the cop can't see us either. We're cloaked." Russell speeds up and cuts the wheel sharp to the right. Through the fog, they suddenly see they're headed towards a row of parked cars. Russell slams on the brakes; tires screech. "Aaaaa!" They scream as the car spins out of control, coming to a halt in the only vacant spot, facing an identical green electric car. They sit panting.

"Forza nothing. I crushed *the game of life!*" Russell cheers.

"Holy crap … "

"Ever notice once you buy a car, all of a sudden you see the same car everywhere?"

"Recalculating …" Iris chirps.

Lights and sirens blaring, the cruiser whizzes by on the main street.

"Holy moly," Will says. "That worked! They drove right past us."

"Return to the route," Iris instructs.

"Oh yeah … mission." Russell slowly pulls out of the parking spot.

"Lights."

"We need to stay cloaked."

"Your destination is ahead," Iris announces.

The car's interior glows red as a siren blares right behind them. Will whips his head around again. "It's an ambulance!" He grabs his chest.

Russell pulls over to let the ambulance go by. The dashboard suddenly flickers, then goes black. Russell repeatedly turns the key. "Oh no, oh no. John's gonna kill me."

"What's wrong?"

"The car won't start."

A black SUV drives past and stops abruptly in front of them.

"Shit … the police," Will says.

"That's not the police."

"Dude, look at the lights."

"No, Willis … look at the No Fear bumper sticker." Russell turns the key again, and the dash comes back to life. The SUV starts moving, and the car lurches forward.

"Dude, what are you doing? Don't follow them."

"I'm not. I'm not driving." Russell's eyes widen. "They got us in a tractor beam!"

"This isn't a movie. Just turn the steering wheel!"

"I am! I am! They locked us in!"

The tires screech when Russell turns the wheel and applies the brakes, but the car continues to lurch ahead.

Russell spies an unfamiliar unit on the roof of the SUV.

"What's that?" He points at it. "I'm telling you: tractor beam!"

The security gate opens, and the SUV turns into the airfield's entrance. The car's tires crackle and pop over the neglected pavement; amidst islands of fog, a large, dark silhouette rises up, interrupting the tree line. The two vehicles drive alongside the arched hangar, headlights rippling across its corrugated tin form.

"This place looks abandoned," Will says.

"Which means no one would think to look for us here."

Iris announces, "You have arrived at your destination."

∘ ∘ ∘

Through the window on the break room door, Lily studies Bill, sitting in his office, head down. She rifles through drawers for anything that might help. She finds a pad of stickie notes and a marker. She peels off a note, flips it over, and writes on the backside:

I keep WJ safe from harm

She slaps the stickie notes on the window facing Bill's office and bangs on the glass until she grabs his attention.

"This is for *your* change purse!" she shouts, then draws directly on the glass, in reverse so he can read:

WAKE UP!

Out of the corner of her eye, a flash of movement in the hangar catches Lily's attention. Pink washes over Infinity, followed by navy blue, then seafoam green.

"Whoa."

Bill limps in, removes the stickie note, crumples it up, and stuffs it in his pants pocket. "I feel like we've gotten off to a bad start."

"What's *that?*" She points through the almost floor-to-ceiling viewing window that overlooks the hangar to Infinity.

Bill grabs a chair. "I'm sure from your point of view I don't look good; I'd draw the same conclusion, but there's a lot you don't know. This isn't how I wanted this to happen, but here we are."

"Your son is thoughtful and compassionate. You should be proud of him."

He takes a deep breath. "You have no idea how hard this is."

"You're not going to hurt me."

"This is an unfortunate situation."

"What *is* that?" Lily nods to Infinity.

"*That* is why you're here, and why my associates are bringing WJ in."

"You're kidnapping your son?"

"*Wake up?* Nice message ... it has Mira written all over it. Where is she?"

Lily glares back. "I don't know who you're talking about."

He slaps his hand on the table. "WJ's life is on the line. Where is she?"

Lily meets his stare with folded arms.

"Believe it or not, I *am* keeping him safe from harm. I'm not the bad guy here." Bill gets up.

"Will won't see it that way."

Bill twists his ring. "For the record, I never wanted to leave him. If I don't open that … whatever it is, we're all dead," he says, returning to his office and closing the blinds.

o o o

The SUV parks next to Janie's sports car behind the hangar; Russell's car stops, and the dash goes dark. Hack and Ash flank the car. Hack taps his phone, and Russell's car's doors unlock.

Ash yanks open the driver's door. "Out," he barks.

"The police will come," Will says.

Hack holds out a black foil-lined bag. "Drop your phones and wallets in the bag please."

"No, they won't," Russell says. "That's a Faraday bag."

Hack flips through Will's wallet. "You look just like your father."

"My father?"

"Welcome to your family reunion, Let's go," Ash says, shoving Will towards the hangar's rear entrance. Ash leads the boys down a short hallway and into the break room. "Which one of you gets the girl, and which is the third wheel?"

Will rushes to Lily. "Are you okay? Did they hurt you?"

"For the record? She's out of both your leagues," Ash says and locks the door.

"I'm fine, but your …"

"Willis," Russell says, "I figured out what your change purse reminded me of."

"What?"

Russell points at Infinity.

"What the heck is that?"

"*E.E.*, Season Two, Episode One: The Franklin Incident."

"What is it?"

"Dude! A UFO! There was this downed craft recovery team … standard above black craft recovery operation. Anyway, one of the guys got too close, and it gobbled him up! They couldn't open fire because they didn't want to hurt him. When he came out, his commanding officer noticed he was acting odd and saying things like, 'I've been such a fool, I finally understand; it's all so clear!' His psych eval showed his IQ had spiked; the drawing in the report looked just like that."

"Why would it look like the change purse?" Lily asks.

"Wrong question," Russell says. "Why would the change purse look like *it?*"

 "We don't know anything about UFOs," Will offers.

"Maybe the A.U. is after you?"

"Don't look at me," Russell says. "I'm just along for the ride."

"Will, it's not Russell the A.U. wants … it's *you.*"

"Me?"

"It's not just the A.U. It's your father. He's here … your father's here."

"My father?"

"He's the one giving the orders."

"Your dad works for the A.U.? Damn, dude. That's messed up."

"Will, he's in trouble …."

Hack opens the door, "Will? Come with me, please."

o o o

"Dad?"

Before a word even escapes his mouth, Bill, limping, charges Will, grabs him by the shirt, and backs him into a corner. "Don't look up," he whispers. "There's a camera. They know you're my son. Go along with me."

Bill pulls Will by the shirt and shoves him into his chair. Will pulls his arms close to his chest. Sitting on the corner of his desk, Bill looms over Will. "Where's Mira?"

"What?"

"You and Lily have been meeting with her." He raises a mug of cold coffee to his lips; it trembles in his hand. "Where is she?"

Will stands in defiant silence.

"I'm not playing games." Bill raises a hand.

Will jumps up into a fight stance, hands in front of him at the ready.

"You're gonna fight me?" Bill says.

"Mom said the bad guys won't let you win. Ever."

"I'm not the bad guy … your mother …"

"Don't you talk about my mother. This is all your fault!"

"WJ, please," Bill rests a hand on Will's shoulder.

"Don't touch me!" Will swats his hand away. "You're A.U. You're the enemy."

Bill shudders then lunges, putting Will in a chokehold. Will stomps on his father's injured foot.

"Aaaa!"

Will pivots, puts Bill in a chokehold, yanks back hard, and the two fall back to the floor.

Ash rushes in and rips the two apart.

"I hate you. I hate you!"

Bill scrambles to his feet.

"Get off me!" In one smooth twist, Will wrestles free and kicks Ash in the groin. Ash doubles over.

"WJ, stop!"

"Come on!" Will shouts.

"I'm warning you, stop it!"

Will spins and lands a hard, open-palmed blow to his father's solar plexus, sending him careening into the desk and knocking the wind out of him.

Ash grabs Will from behind.

"Get off me!"

"Your piss ant kid needs to learn to respect his elders."

"He's not my father!" Panting heavily, Will glares at Bill.

Bill regains his breath. "Put him in with the girl," he says, rubbing his chest, and Ash escorts Will back across the hall.

"I found something you might want to see," Hack offers Wen's business card to Bill.

"Consciousness Trainer," Bill turns the card over. "Where did you find this?"

"From the boy's … I mean your son's wallet." Hack gently places the wallet on the desk. "I can't imagine how you must be feeling. I'm so sorry …."

"Why is the car charging?"

"Deb's recharging, we used her to apprehend the boys."

"You used Deb on *my son?*"

"It wasn't me …."

"That damn Directed Energy Beam almost killed my family! Ash!" he hollers.

"Yeah?"

"You used that damn thing on my son?"

"Yeah, you got a problem with that?"

"That's my son!" Bill swings and lands a punch on Ash's jaw.

"Sucker punched by baby hands." Ash checks his jaw.

"That damned thing almost killed my family!"

Hack jumps between them. "Mr. E … it was my idea to use Deb. Your son was never in danger. We didn't push, we pulled the boys."

"Boys? How many boys?"

"Your son and his friend, Russell Laforce … here's his wallet."

"And you're telling me this now?" Bill raises the venetian blind and sees Will, Russell, and Lily in the break room.

"Unbelievable." Bill shakes his head. He grabs the card between his index and pointer fingers and holds it out for Ash. "Here's your next assignment. Get Wen."

Ash snatches the card, turns, and puts his fist through the door's glass window. "Brings back memories, don't it?" The glass crunches beneath Ash's boots as he leaves. "Your kid hits harder than you."

"Don't worry about that, Mr. E, I'll take care of it." Hack closes the door on his way out, then sticks a hand through the shattered window, locates the drawstring with his fingers, and lets down the blind.

Bill turns over Will's wallet and caresses it. The colorful paper billfold was the Miyazaki wallet Mary bought him as a souvenir of their summer family outing to Boston. She found it in a Japanese Anime store. It was a sweet reminder of the animated movies the three enjoyed together. He never got a chance to transfer his belongings from his old wallet; she bought it just days before he was ripped away; now, it belonged to Will.

Opening it, he pulls out Will's student ID; it's the first picture of his son he's seen in twelve years. His cheeks aren't chubby anymore, and Will's once silken hair is now that of a young man; darker, thick, and tousled across his forehead. He reminds Bill of a young Rob Lowe. Glancing at the wallet, a bit of colored paper tucked behind the student ID catches his eye. He tugs on the hand-cut paper copy of an old photo taken when Will turned three.

"Let me get this! Let me get this!" His mother held the camera close and ... Click. *"I got it!"*

"Mary ..." Bill mutters.

He stares deeply into the photo of the two of them; a tear lands on Will's ID.

SEVENTEEN

Get Wen

"Would you pass me that cable?"

Ash sets down his tobacco tin and grabs a cable off the floor for Hack. Hack flips on his phone's flashlight and patches his server into the router. He turns off the flashlight, leaving the two in the only light in the windowless utility van, the eerie glow of computer monitors. Hack clacks on his keyboard as he studies his bank of displays. Ash stuffs a bit of chaw in his cheek; looking like a hulking chipmunk, he hunches over Hack and studies the displays.

"You're gonna get cancer. I wish you'd quit."

"Do I tell you how to live your life?"

Hack inserts his earpiece, "Testing, testing. Mr. E, is your laptop receiving our feeds? Can you hear me?"

"Loud and clear," Bill's tinny voice comes back. "Ash, your body cam is pointed to the ground." Ash adjusts his camera. "Thanks," Bill answers.

Hack spins in his chair, leans over, and opens a large suitcase containing a half-dozen drones.

"That's quite a case of hemorrhoids you've got there," Ash snickers.

"How long have you been working on that one?"

"Just show me where she is … I'll do the real work." Ash wipes black greasepaint on his face, completing his nighttime tactical outfit.

Hack opens the back doors, and with a few taps on his phone, four drones *bleep* to life, unfurl their props, and launch themselves out and up into the air, coming to a halt just beneath the power lines. A wandering raccoon takes notice. A few more taps on his phone, and the drones drift silently across the road towards 1111 Eleventh St. Ash looks on as each takes up a flanking position along a different wall.

"One minute … collating …" Hack says.

Ash spits out the rear of the van. "Your toys better give me the edge."

"Here we go … I got a visual."

"Me too." Ash watches as the Roid to the left of the building fires its scanning lasers into a second-story window.

The laser scans Mira's bedroom, casting her room in amber monochrome. Through the parted curtains, the beam strikes a crystal sun-catcher; a burst of amber diamonds sprays the room. R4 rotates in place for a better look at her sleeping form.

"Inoperable," Mira says. Like a stone tossed into a pond, the drone drops to the ground below.

"What the ..." Hack checks the diagnostics. "R4 just went dark."

"Your sinker dropped into the toilet."

"That's impossible ... they're charged ... her diagnostics were spot on. I saw her; she was asleep, then it cut off."

"Send another one."

"She might have jamming tech ... I can't protect the roids against unknown threats."

"Great, so I'm going in blind?"

"We've still got three other eyes on the house."

Turning to Hack's monitors, Ash studies the green-on-black 3D layout of the building. "What's that red blob?"

"Another heat signature."

"Her?"

"No, a second one."

Ash hops out of the van. "Final count?" He unsleeves his rifle.

"A gun? You heard Mr. E ... you mustn't hurt her."

"Relax, it's a tranq."

"Mr. E ..."

"I approved it, Hack. Trust me, it won't hurt her ... these are the short-sleep darts; she'll be out long enough for us to bag her."

Ash inspects his rifle's night scope; scanning pitch-black bushes, he locates a well-lit, green-tinged raccoon.

"Perfect. If I wanted, I could take out that raccoon at the fifty-yard line."

"You're barbaric."

"Grow a pair."

"Stay focused!" Bill scolds.

"What's my final count?"

"Two."

"Let's move out."

Hack grabs a zippered leather kit from a bin and opens it.

"What are you doing?"

"Double checking my kit … not sure what kind of lock she has." Hack zips it up and stuffs it in a vest pocket.

"Can we go now, Claudine?"

"What a sizable spider crawling up your leg!"

Ash jumps back and spins in a circle as he slaps frantically at his pants leg.

"Gotcha–Spiderman."

"Can the two of you stay focused for more than a minute?"

"Sorry, Mr. E … we're moving out," Hack says and pries Ash's hands off his jacket. Hack moves to take a step towards the house, and Ash trips him.

With only moonlight to guide them, the two sneak across the street and tiptoe up the front steps. Crouching in front of the door, Hack grabs his kit. Working like a dentist, he inserts two metal picks into the lock and moves them around.

His back against the wall, Ash waits, hugging his rifle close to his chest.

"We're in."

Click ka-chunk. The door swings open. "Can I help you?"

Hack looks up. Above the plaid PJ pants and his sports T-shirt with an a.i.e. team logo, Joe stares back. Ash spins into the doorway and swings; Joe deftly dodges the butt of his rifle, tosses something in Ash's face, and disappears into the dark house.

"Aargh, sand! Punk move."

"What do I do?"

"Go after him!" Ash orders, rubbing his eyes.

"Do I look like a Navy Seal?"

"I'm compromised! Get eyes on him, get eyes on him!"

"I'm going as fast as I can!" Hack frantically taps on his phone, and a Roid flies past them into the house.

"You're sending a Roid?" Ash opens his bloodshot eyes wide.

"Use your eyes! Dammit … just tell me where he went, I'll find him myself."

Hack swipes at his phone. "Bloody hell, R1 lost him!"

"Which way did he go?"

"Aren't we here for the woman?"

"They're working together… and now I got a score to settle. Which way did he go?"

"Straight through there …" Hack points past the parlor.

A one-man tactical force, Ash hugs the walls as he makes his way through the foyer into the parlor. He silently sprints across the dark room to just outside the conservatory; Hack apes Ash's moves from a few steps behind.

"I'm picking up a smaller heat signature," Hack whispers.

"Dog?" Ash flicks on his scope's green targeting laser.

"Too high." Hack points up in the tree, cast in silver by moonlight. "It's hiding in the branches; just thermal, no visual. A large bird?"

Ash spins into the doorway. Sparrows, stirred from their slumber, squawk like barn animals before a storm. Ash circumnavigates the tree, one eye trained in his night vision scope; the rifle's targeting laser lights up pine needles; dust floats in and out of the green laser light like feisty fairies. The laser dot lands on feathers. Through the scope, he sees two glowing eyes staring back at him. A branch jostles; Ash fires. Screeching like a bewitched cat, a great horned owl swoops down and swipes at Ash with his talons. "Shit!" The green laser dances in the conservatory as Ash flails at the darkness; he sprints directly into the tree and lands flat on his back.

"It's an owl!" Hack hisses as the animal flies past him and out the front door.

"No shit, sherlock."

From the top of the parlor stairs, Mira interrupts them. "Are you looking for me?"

Hack spins around. "Master Wen?"

"Old business cards," she says.

Ash leans against the conservatory entryway to stabilize his shot. "What the hell Bill? It's *her!* You didn't tell me she's the target. I'm taking the shot."

"Stop!" Hack grabs the barrel of Ash's rifle and aims it away from Mira.

Ash lets go of his rifle, letting it dangle from its shoulder strap, draws his handgun, and presses its muzzle to Hack's forehead. "You're jeopardizing the mission!"

"Ash, what the hell are you doing?"

"I can confirm, Mr. E," Hack stares down Ash, "our security officer is pointing a gun at me."

"Stand down, Ash!" Bill's voice yells into Ash's earpiece.

"Let me take the shot!" Ash demands.

"She's unarmed, you baboon!"

"Bill, I need to take the shot *now!* I can shoot Hack or her. Pick one."

"I said stand down and lower your weapon!" Bill orders. "You blow this for me, and I will put a bullet in your skull myself!"

"Neanderthal has lowered his firearm."

"Hack, is she still there?" Bill asks.

"Yes, I'm still here," Mira calls down.

Ash raises his rifle and shoves Hack out of the way.

"Ash, let Hack bring her in … Ash?... Ash?..."

"Copy that," Ash mutters, keeping Mira framed in his scope.

"Master Wen, my apologies for the intrusion. We are in urgent need of your services. I'm Hack, and this is …"

"Ash and I have met." She turns to Ash. "Like Mr. Hack said, put down your gun so you can talk like civilized humans."

"I'll put it down when you're in the van."

"Master Wen, allow me to explain …."

"You don't need to explain; I'm aware of the situation."

"Then you'll come?"

"When Ash puts down the rifle."

"Be a good girl. Come downstairs and hop in the van," Ash responds.

"Is that how you talk to Janie?"

"We can do this the hard way or the easy way." The green line connects Ash's rifle to Wen's chest, marking her tank top with a bright green spot.

"The easy way isn't always the best way," she says.

The house lights come on all at once, overloading Ash's night scope and blinding him.

"Aaah!" Ash shuts his eyes and looks away.

"Where did she go?" He lowers his rifle, shading his eyes and squinting.

"She's gone!"

"I know that! Which way? Left or right?"

Hack swipes through his phone. "She … she just vanished!"

Ash presses at his earpiece. "The package is gone!"

"Good."

"Good?"

"She's coming for me; get back here."

"Get to the van!" Ash barks, tossing Hack the keys.

"Yikes, you're bleeding. That owl did a number on your face."

"Suck it up, buttercup. It's just a scratch." Ash swipes his bloody right cheek with his left forearm and pulls out his phone.

"You're texting? You can't use unsecured channels."

"Mind your own business."

"I'm serious. Do you want our presence here to be tracked?"

"It won't matter." Ash sends a single text: "It's happening."

"Who are you texting?"

"Mind your business and drive."

∘ ∘ ∘

The whine of the hangar's industrial lighting is momentarily interrupted by the crackle of flickering lights.

"Look!" Lily taps Will on the arm and points out the window.

"Mira!" As Mira proceeds towards them the two pound on the glass.

"No, Mira! Go back!" Will yells. "Get out of here! Run!"

"Who's that?" Russell asks.

Mira walks straight up to the window. Head cocked, she puts her hand up to the glass.

"Mira, go get help!" Will screams.

As though she were slipping into pool water, Mira's hand pushes straight through the glass; then she walks through the glass wall.

Lily gasps and reaches for Will's hand as the two step back.

Russell points at Mira, mouth agape.

"How did you do that?" Will asks. "Do you have some sort of device?"

"I am the device. It's best if none of you tell anyone what you just saw."

Russell leaps to his feet, wipes a hand against his pants, and holds it out to greet her. "Master Wen, it's an honor."

"That's not Wen; that's Mira," Will corrects.

"Expectation … we haven't gotten to that yet. Nice to meet

you, Russell."

"She knows my name!" Russell glows.

"Mira … Wen?" Lily points to Infinity. "Will's father wants you to open that."

"I know … call me Wen."

"Hello, Wen," Bill says from the doorway.

"I'm here. You've got what you wanted."

"Let us go," Will demands.

"I'm still your father."

"You wish. My father would never let this happen."

Bill scratches his finger.

Wen grabs his hand. "Perhaps it's time to take off that ring?"

"Mr. Krone will kill every one of us if I don't open that," Bill says.

"Will, come here," Wen says.

"Leave him alone! Don't pull my son into this."

"They took the wrong Freeman," Wen says. "Bill, I was hoping you would see that on your own. Perhaps things happened this way for a reason. Will, I would like you to quiet your mind."

"Wen, I'm not good at this."

"We gave you those dreams to help you remember your true nature."

"You gave me *dreams?*"

"We give lots of people dreams. A few listen."

"Wait … it was you standing with the others… by the pond… in my dream. I saw you. I saw all of you."

"You have the capacity."

"You were the one who kept defending me."

"Because I believe in you. This knowledge is meant to be shared. Will, you can open it."

"What about him?" Will points to his father. "He trained for this."

"No, he was trained for *you.*"

Will looks at his father.

"This is not how I imagined today would go," Bill says.

"Bill … Intention." Wen says. "In your heart of hearts, how do you want this to turn out?"

Lily takes Will's hand. "Will, you got this."

"Listen to the Master. I believe in you too, bro."

"What about Mr. Krone? If I do this, will he stop coming after us?"

"He cannot harm you."

"You don't know that," Bill snaps.

"Will,"—Wen nods to Infinity—"focus your attention on her. Hold the intention of communicating and the expectation of success."

With a deep inhale, then exhale, Will closes his eyes and relaxes his face. Instinctively, he raises a hand.

"Does that help?" Russell whispers to Lily. "Holding up a hand?"

"Shhh!" Lily presses a finger to her lips.

Russell, Lily, and Bill all hold their breath. Iridescent pulses of color wash over Infinity as her rigid structure softens.

"Will Freeman."

Who are you?

"I am Infinity."

Bloop, bloop, bloop, bloop.

The sound engulfs the hangar. Like a Venus flytrap resetting, Infinity slowly opens along her topmost seam.

"Beautiful," Hack says from the hallway.

Bill spins around. Past Hack, he sees Ash crouched behind the desk in Bill's office, rifle aimed at Wen. "No!" Bill shouts. Wen pushes Will behind her.

Bang!

With a pinch of her thumb and forefinger, Wen catches the dart in midair. Infinity closes.

"No, no, no, no!" Bill cries out.

Stunned, Ash lowers his rifle.

"You fool! We had it opened!" Bill yells.

"She's a threat," Ash sneers.

"She's here! Your services aren't needed, so just sit down and keep your mouth shut."

"If I open this again, can we go home?" Will says.

"It's not that simple," Bill says.

"I'm not talking about you," Will says. "Can *me and my friends* go home if I open it again?"

"Listen, kid," Ash says, "it's not up to your father."

"He's not my father!" Will pushes past the adults and marches out of the break room right up to Infinity, then extends his palm. Under his hand, waves of color pulse out across Infinity's surface. Like a giant mollusk, Infinity again opens for him. Pale blue translucent nubs emerge from the gap. Lengthening tubules find Will and wind around him.

Will turns to Bill. "Dad?"

Will goes limp, Infinity yanks him inside, retreats into her shell, and snaps shut.

"No!" Bill wails as he, Lily, and Russell rush to Infinity.

Ash cuts them off. "Everybody get back!"

"Wen!" Bill turns around. "Where's Wen?"

"Master Wen is in there," Russell points to Infinity.

∘ ∘ ∘

A nine-foot-tall grizzly looms behind Mr. Krone. Staged in ferocity, teeth bared and its large right paw swiping the air, it is only an imaginary threat. His Trophy Room is filled with dozens of creatures, hollowed-out and posed, the centerpiece being a large bull elk, standing triumphant surrounded by a pack of fallen wolves. Glassy eyes focus on Mr. Krone's crown of silvery hair lit from above. Oblivious to his butler, Mr. Krone hangs his head like a vulture waiting for his prey to fall. He dabs at the drool in the corner of his mouth. His eyes greedily follow the late-night reality show unfolding on his laptop: teenagers yelling on Camera 3.

"More coffee, sir?"

"Master Wen." Spittle clings to his parched lips as he speaks. He watches as Mira walks through the hangar on Camera 1. He reaches for his coffee; his eyes are glued to the screen as she places her hand on the viewing window.

The video feed flickers. "Dammit!" Mr. Krone splashes coffee on his silk pajamas, and the feeds resume. "Dammit! How'd she get in there?"

On Camera 6, a windowless van pulls up to the back of the building, and Hack and Ash spring out. "The cavalry has arrived." He turns up the volume when Ash grabs Hack by the shoulder.

"We tried your way, and she got away, so now we're doing it my way. Here's how it's gonna go …"—he turns off his rifle's laser sight—"if she's in there, you're not gonna touch my rifle, you're not gonna snitch to anyone, you're gonna keep your mouth *shut,* and you're gonna let me take the shot. Got it?"

"If she's in there, doesn't that mean my way worked?"

Ash shakes his head.

"Why shoot?" Hack asks.

"Because she's a demon, that's why."

"You got that right," Mr. Krone lowers his voice as he watches them stealthily enter through the back door.

"Mr. Krone will kill every one of us if I don't open that," Bill pleads to Wen.

"You don't know the half of me," Mr. Krone slurps his coffee.

"Leave him alone! Don't pull my son into this."

"They took the wrong Freeman."

On Camera 2, Ash slips into Bill's office. His back against the wall, he turns and peers into the break room, pulling back when Mira turns her head.

"Jesus, don't let her see you!" Mr. Krone hisses directions like an armchair quarterback.

On Camera 4, Hack is crouched in the hallway just behind the doors, with a view of the hangar and Infinity.

"In your heart of hearts, how do you want this to turn out?"

"I know exactly how I want this to turn out," Mr. Krone comments.

"What about Mr. Krone? If I do this, will he stop coming after us?"

"He cannot harm you."

"You don't know that," Mr. Krone and Bill both say.

Back on Camera 2, Ash is crouched behind Bill's desk. Like he was crowning a house of cards, he carefully rests the pistol grip on the desk.

Will raises a hand.

"Does that help?" Mr. Krone asks, along with Russell. He leans in as iridescent waves wash over Infinity's surface.

Bloop, bloop, bloop, bloop.

Infinity opens.

He zooms the camera. Its insides are fleshy.

"He's done it!" Mr. Krone howls with delight.

"Beautiful."

"No!"

Bang!

Wen snatches the dart, and Infinity shuts.

"You fool! We had it opened!" Bill yells.

"Jesus, Ash, you're good for just one thing!" Mr. Krone snaps at the screen.

"She's here!" Bill rails. "Your services aren't needed, so just sit down and keep your mouth shut."

"Kick him in the balls for me," Mr. Krone grimaces.

"I'm not talking about you. Can *me and my friends* go home if I open it again?"

"Listen, kid," Ash says, "it's not up to your father."

"He's my not father!"

"Give him hell, boy." Mr. Krone says. "Give them all hell."

Will marches out of Camera 3; Mr. Krone zooms out of Camera 1.

"You got it," he encourages as Will raises his hand again. "You got it …."

Mr. Krone holds his breath as Infinity's tubules reach around like vines in time-lapse.

"Go with it," he says as tubules wrap themselves around Will.

"Dad?" Will goes limp, and Infinity pulls him in and closes.

"I'll be damned. The kid did it. He's in!"

"Simon! Bring the car around!" Mr. Krone stands up so fast that his chair nearly topples the heron behind him. "And don't wake my driver. I'm going for a drive."

EIGHTEEN

Transformation

"Stop!" Hack yells. "There's a child in that car!"

Ash flips the wipers to maximum.

"Try the Directed Energy Beam."

"Mr. Krone, sir, using Deb could be lethal."

"What good is it if I can't use it?"

"Sir, my device …"

"No … my device."

"Sir …"

"Do it."

Hack feels the sweat on his fingers as he pulls a remote out of the glove compartment. With a button press, a circular panel rises up atop the vehicle. "Ugh," Hack frowns at the blob in the remote's video feed. "There's something blocking the camera, pull over!"

"I'm not stopping."

"Would you slow down, at least? I need to clear the

obstruction." Hack opens his window; he grabs the car's wet frame and sits precariously on the open window. The rain stings his face; he turns his head away so he can open his eyes. The wind presses a rain-soaked leaf against the rooftop camera lens. His shoes sinking into the seat, he palms the windshield with one hand while reaching for the leaf with the other. "Whoa!" The car lurches into the wake of an eighteen-wheeler passing in the other direction. Hack's hand slips off of the windshield. Just as he feels himself falling back, something catches him; Ash's tattooed fist grips his shirt; he holds onto Hack until he regains his balance.

Hack takes a deep breath and reaches again for the leaf. "Got it!" Like a wet mop, he flops back in his seat, and Ash steps on the gas.

"It worked. I can see now." Hack rotates the power dial on the remote all the way down, lines up Bill's car in the display with the joystick, and presses PUSH.

Vvvrrowm.

Ash glances over. "You missed."

"No, I hit them."

"Hit 'em harder."

"I don't like this …."

Vvvrrowmmmmmmmmm!

The sound rattles their windows.

"Harder!"

"They could've crashed!"

"That's the point."

"Let's keep Bill alive, shall we?" Mr. Krone chimes in.

"I'm not having a child's blood on my hands!"

"Gimme that!" Ash snatches the remote from Hack. "Grab the wheel."

"I won't be a party to this." Hack crosses his drenched arms.

Ash takes his other hand off the wheel; skipping on each puddle, the car veers into opposing traffic.

"You're insane!" Hack shouts, grabbing the wheel.

"And you're British." Ash turns the dial to maximum.

"Please … DON'T …"

"Just like a video game …."

VVVRROWMMMMMMMMM!

"Oh, God!" Hack shields his eyes as they pass the car careening into the ditch.

Bloop. Like a video on fast forward, the scene quickly shifts.

"You just earned your wings." Ash tosses Bill off the hood.

"Welcome to the A.U." He drags Bill like a poached animal in shock to their vehicle and stuffs him into the back seat next to Mr. Krone.

"No witnesses …" Mr. Krone tells Ash.

Bill's face—rain-soaked, bloody, swollen, and gashed— is unrecognizable. "No!" he groans. "Don't you touch my family!"

"Shut up," Ash punches Bill's pulpy face, grabs his pistol from under his suit, and marches back towards the crumpled car. From the bottom of the ditch, Mary stares back, Holding WJ tight.

Ash raises the pistol at her.

A bright blue light forms between Ash and Mary; a luminous woman emerges. "Leave them!" she commands. Ash aims the pistol at her.

Click.

Ash works to clear the jam in the chamber. "Aah!" He passes the gun from hand to hand; rain striking the gun evaporates in pungent steam. He drops the overheated weapon on the street. Despite the driving rain, the gun glows red hot, bursts into flames, and crumbles.

Struck dumb, Ash turns and runs.

NINETEEN

The Birth of Will Freeman

Will sits bolt upright, throwing off his bedsheets. "Was all that just a dream? Or is *this?*" He picks up his pillow and sniffs it; tossing it aside, he turns his attention to the floor. Leading with his foot, he pushes his laundry; his father's studded belt flops out of the pile. Will steps over it to get a closer look at his stereo; the album and photo are right where he and Lily left them. Everything is in its place; his room seems completely ordinary.

"Wait. Curtains?" His long-gone outer space curtains billow into his room. *"Mom!"*

Bloop.

"Is it my move again?"

"Did you put my curtains back?"

"Looks like it's curtains for your queen,"—his mom lets go of her knight. "Hey, I never asked … how did your date with Lily go?"

Bloop.

Will swoons at Lily's impish grin.

"Will he or won't he?" Lily says as she closes her eyes, puckers her lips, and leans in.

Will shakes his head. "This isn't real."

Bloop.

"That's just like you, isn't it? You wouldn't believe something if it smacked you in the face."

"Oscar!" Will's doppelgänger looms over him.

"Remember me?"

"You're not real. I got rid of you."

"You can't get rid of me that easy," Oscar pushes Will, and he tumbles backward off the cliff.

Falling, he feels warm air pushing upwards against his left hand. Will dives into the thermal; the cushion of rising air reverses his fall, pushing him, like an invisible magic carpet, high above the cliffside and Oscar. The ocean stretches in front of him; Will slips off the thermal and glides his way to a tropical island; everything fades.

"Hello, Will."

"Who's there?"

"I am Infinity."

"Where are you?"

"Here, with you."

"I can't see you."

"How's this?"

As if on a stage, lights bump up. A woman with the beauty

and glamor of a Golden Era film star steps forward. She wears a silky emerald dress and heels. A handful of well-placed broad, blonde curls nestle around her neck. She takes Will's hand, and—accompanied by a big band swing score—they dance, gracefully twirling their way up a spiral ramp. Will notices her hair tie has the same Celtic knot as Lily's. He catches a glimpse of her face, she looks like she could be Lily as an adult. They dance into darkness.

"How did you do that?"

"Will, that was all you. You wanted to see me, so there I was."

"I saw a bunch of stuff before … my bedroom, Mom, Lily, Oscar. Am I dead?"

"You're very much alive. You were reflecting on what you love."

"What about Oscar?"

"Oscar is part of you."

"I saw the car accident … is that what really happened?"

"Yes."

"I didn't know."

"Perspective is freeing."

Bloop.

Bill scratches a ticket outside a grocery store. "I won $1,111!" he tugs excitedly at a passerby.

"There's something in the air today … I just won the same amount." The passerby shows Bill his winning ticket.

"What are the odds? Must be a million to one!"

"I'm Joe," they shake hands.

Bloop.

WJ let go with both hands and stretched both arms out. He saw his father's large hands beneath his outstretched arms, ready to catch him.

"Look at you … you're flying!"

WJ remembered the freedom of that moment in flight and how his father supported him.

"Let me get this! Let me get this!" His mother held the camera close and … *Click.* "I got it!"

Bloop.

"You caught me when I'm feeling generous," Mr. Krone tells Bill. "You know what? You can have them back, even if you don't open it."

"Really?"

"I'll just change your cot into bunk beds. Or, I could just have you all killed."

Bloop.

"You're gonna fight me?"

"Mom said the bad guys won't let you win," Will says. "Ever."

"I'm not the bad guy … your mother …"

"Don't you talk about my mother. This is all your fault!"

"WJ, please," Bill goes to rest a hand on Will's shoulder.

"Don't touch me!" Will swats his hand away. "You're A.U. You're the enemy."

Bloop.

"Judgement is a burden."

"I didn't know he was kidnapped … it wasn't his choice … Infinity, I had no idea."

"You have the capacity."

"I judged him without knowing the truth. It was so easy to be angry at him. All this time, I wanted him to suffer … he was already suffering; all my anger did was make us both suffer. I have to help him," Will wipes tears from his cheek with the back of his hand. A soft glow enwraps him. He is suddenly surrounded by thousands of pale, luminescent change purses. Like a child in a ball pit, he clambers to get out but sinks deeper.

"Hello, Will."

"Mira … I'm sinking!"

"Are you sinking? Or are you surrounded by possibilities?"

Chest deep and still descending, he asks frantically, "What do I do? What do I do?"

"You have the capacity."

"Wen!" He thrusts a hand towards her and holds his breath as his nose passes below the surface. It felt like he was underwater, surrounded by a school of jellyfish. Unable to hold his breath any longer, he lets out his air and inhales deeply.

I can breathe.

He sinks into the murky water as air bubbles flow out through his nose, and he lands on a soft, dark ledge. His hands press against it as he pushes himself upward, but the ledge moves slowly beneath him. The massive moving dark wall belongs to a whale. It suddenly stops. Its large eye meets Will's gaze, and the two stare in silence at each other.

"Wooo! Wooo. Wooo." The whale calls out to him and then, like a cruise ship pulling out of dock, moves forward slowly. Will watches the whale glide past him in majestic silence, no ripples, not even a bubble. "Wooo! Wooo. Wooo." The whale calls to Will once more. It flips its tail in the water, and Will watches the whale head towards the surface.

A far-off blue light catches Will's attention. Lights and outlines take the shape of an underwater city. Will blinks to make sure his eyes aren't deceiving him. It's still there. He sees it! In the glow of a city, another world exists.

Wen's words to his father float into his thoughts. "In your heart of hearts, how do you want this to turn out?"

Is this what Wen wanted me to know? To see?—Wen! I have to tell Wen.

Will starts swimming upwards; a cold, firm hand grabs at his ankle.

"He has the capacity." The words of the council wash into his mind.

Will jerks his leg away.

"Fail!" Oscar says, grabbing Will's other ankle.

"No, you failed!" Will thrashes. "Didn't you hear them? I have the capacity."

"Listen to me. I can protect you! Listen to me!"

"No!" Will jerks violently in the water to free himself.

"Will, don't leave me!" Oscar pleads as his fingers desperately grasp at Will's ankles.

Like a boulder tossed into the water, the whale splashes in front of Will. Its force pushes Will up and away from Oscar. Will looks up, and the sea of purses above him parts; wavering light from above shines a clear path to Wen. Another breach of the whale tosses Will out of the water. He lands in the purse pit with Wen.

"Oh my God, did you see that whale?!"

"Yes."

"And the city! I saw a city!"

"Yes, and you saw it with good reason. I knew you were the one."

"The night of the accident, when Mom said she saw an angel, it was you, wasn't it? And you were the one who kept defending me."

"Because I knew you are the one we have been looking for. There was only one person who could open Infinity and have the clarity of vision to see another world. And if you can see that world, you can help others see a better world here. You are the one."

Will's face lights up. "What is your real name? Is it Mira or Wen?"

"Wen."

"Wen? Does your name mean something?"

"It means to ask. If you want clarity, ask. You no longer have to listen to Oscar. You are not alone, Will Freeman." She hovers a hand over the change purses. "You and I are more alike than you think."

The ground under their feet becomes firm, and Infinity's shell becomes sheer; the hangar shimmers with color. Streams of light form a vast network, connecting everything to everything else, coalescing and intersecting around people.

"What's happening out there? Everyone's frozen," Will says.

"Time passes differently in here."

"Whoa— everything looks so strange." Blips of color zip around, blurring the edges of people's forms.

"New perspectives can be overwhelming the first time."

"Other people have been in here?"

"You're not the first."

"Where are they?"

"They have returned to their lives. They were not ready to help."

"Help with what?"

"You need an upgrade."

"Me?"

"Everyone."

"Oh … " Will thinks. "Wen, I'm not ready to help with that either. I'm just me; I'm ordinary."

Wen points to the frozen scene in the hangar. "What you are seeing is multifaceted: what you are capable of seeing, what you are ready to see, and what you believe to be true."

"What are those dark splotches around Ash?"

"Suppressed fears," Infinity's voice surrounds them.

"That guy? What could he possibly be afraid of?"

Bloop.

"Daddy!"

"What?"

"There's a spider in my room!" Pulling his father by a finger, Dickie points to the shag carpet. "What's that white ball it's got?"

"Babies … hundreds. Stomp on it!"

"I don't want to!"

"Don't be a baby."

Pulling its clutch of eggs, the mother spider inches closer to freedom under Dickie's bed.

"It's getting away!"

Ash's father picks up little Dickie and holds him over the spider. "Stomp it, or you'll have baby spiders in your ears tonight."

"Put me down! Put me down!"

"Okay …"

Dickie tumbles to the floor. Peeling his hand off the rug, he shrieks at the grisly scene on his palm— a badly maimed spider and a smushed clutch.

"You scream like a girl."

Bloop.

Will winces from Ash's childhood memory.

"Appearing weak," Wen answers. "That's what he fears."

"What are the lines coming off people?"

"Connections."

"Ash has lines connecting to Hack," Will says. "And Lily!"

"Envy."

"Envy?" Will says. "Ash?"

"He's ashamed, so he hides it … just like he hides his fear. He hides his feelings so well he's hidden them from himself." Wen turns to Will. "Let's try something different. Think about your mother; where is she?"

"I see her! There's literally a cloud over her head."

"Worry."

"You're seeing in metaphor. Now bring your attention back to the hangar."

"Look at Russell," Will says. "He's glowing."

"Self-confidence."

Will turns his attention to his father. Lines move in, around, and out of his body. They connect Bill to the photo on his desk, the wallet in his drawer, his coffee mug, and the microwave. Countless lines of different colors stretch beyond the walls; the sturdiest white line, thick as an anchor's rope, goes straight into Will's chest. The sturdiest black line goes out past the hangar walls.

Bloop.

The butler's white-gloved hands hold Mr. Krone's chair securely on the Persian rug as he sits.

"Thank you, Simon," Mr. Krone nods to his three guests, and they take their seats. The opulent, mahogany-walled dining room looks like a replica of a room from Versailles. Ornate gold frames adorn large mirrors and masterpieces. Floral arrangements larger than an umbrella add ornament to marble-topped sideboards. Topiaries and potted palms soften the edges of the room, while floor-to-ceiling windows look out across the terrace; past that, a seemingly endless stretch of French Renaissance-style gardens. In the distance, a peacock struts across the lawn. Simon nods to the maids: one pours mimosas while another begins serving the meal.

"Mitzi, you're so far away." Bruno whines, his olive complexion making him the darkest one in the room. "You're missing the view of the gardens."

"No, Bruno,"—she says from the far end of the table—"I've secured my front-row seat to the show." She motions to the maid to fill her champagne flute to the rim.

"Simon, where's August?" Mr. Krone asks.

"He is in the Empire Suite closing on the Minsk deal, sir."

"They've been in there for hours. How often do I share a meal with all my children?" The maid flattens his napkin across his lap. "Simon, tell him his business is in here." Another maid serves Mr. Krone his game hen.

"Yes, sir."

"Father, we're here," Bruno offers.

Mr. Krone stabs a fork into his hen and slices off a piece of breast. "The three of you will have to do."

"Father, a gallery in Milan has expressed interest in showing my work ..." Hedy leans back while the maid places her napkin for her.

"... and she wants money," Mitzi says.

"It's very prestigious! It's the recognition I've been looking for," Hedy defends.

"Hedy, it's rude to ask for money at the table." He drops his knife and fork, grabs a drumstick, and rips it off.

"I haven't asked for money, Father!"

"Yet," Mitzi interjects between gulps. "These mimosas are weak."

Her father glares down the table at her.

"What's wrong, Father? Am I embarrassing myself again? How uncouth of me."

"You're making a fool of yourself," Hedy chides.

"The Fool says what no one else dares. I may always be the baby in this family, but this baby has common sense and a modicum of human decency." Mitzi counters.

"For God's sake Mitzi," Bruno interjects. "You're in his house, at his table, drinking his booze and eating his food. The least you can do is show some respect."

Mitzi rolls her eyes. "How ironic: he's got all the money in the world, but he still can't buy a nickel's worth of respect."

"Glug, glug," Hedy mimes chugging a bottle, then wiping her mouth on her sleeve.

"Why do you think I drink?" Mitzi asks.

Mr. Krone scowls at his daughters. "What have you made of yourselves?"

A built-in bookcase swings open. August marches through the secret door, pen and papers in hand.

"I need your signature on these."

"August, you're late, and I'm eating. It can wait."

"No, it can't. They're leaving in ten minutes."

"I'm not feeling well; I need my heart medicine."

"Simon," August says, "bring my father his heart medicine."

"No, August. You get it."

"We don't have time for this. If I were Board Chair, I'd be done by now."

"I will make you Chair when you've demonstrated that you're up to the job. Until then, fetch me my heart medicine."

August spins on his heels. "Out of my way!" He snaps at the maids on his way out.

"Fetch? *Fetch?*" Mitzi interjects. "You use etiquette to broadcast how refined you are, but you treat August like a dog. Why can't we be like a normal family?"

"You want normal? Give me back your $120,000 Benz and buy yourself a Prius." He shoves a forkful of oyster stuffing into his mouth. "Mind your manners, girl." Stuffing sputters onto the table.

"Did you just spit food on your Louis XVI table while lecturing me about manners? Now that's some blue blood bullshit."

"You're insufferable." Mr. Krone changes the subject. "Bruno."

"Yes, Father?"

"August tells me you're selling Helsinki."

"Yes, I'm working on it," Bruno rearranges his silverware.

"It's not done yet? August would have had it done weeks ago."

"The buyer is making demands. This sale requires patience."

"Patience?"

"I'm establishing a long-term relationship with them; I'm exercising diplomacy."

"Bruno, God gave you eyes to see humanity, ears to hear wisdom, a heart to feel compassion, and a brain to know better than to listen to all of that. Grab them by the balls, and close the damn deal."

August marches back in and slaps a pill on the table. "Here's your damned medicine."

"The prodigal son has returned," Mitzi rolls the stem of her glass between her thumb and forefinger.

"Now, please sign this!"

"And he brings *paperwork!*"

"This so-called *paperwork* will net Father $500 million. What have you brought to the table ... besides your noxious, alcoholic tongue?"

Mr. Krone washes his pill down with his Bloody Mary, signs the paperwork, and hands the pen back to August. "Now sit and eat with me. The company at this table is dreadful."

Hedy, Bruno, and Mitzi exchange glances.

"You're nothing but daddy's little wooden-headed dummy," Mitzi says. "You haven't a thought of your own."

"Worthless. You were right, Father." He leaves through the bookcase.

Mitzi's shoulders drop. "So, Father, you do think I'm worthless?" She casts her eyes down the long table; Mr. Krone is silent. A tear streams down her cheek, dropping to her napkin before she can wipe it from her face. She tosses her napkin on the table and downs the last of her mimosa. "I can't believe I wore my good Louis Vuitton's for this." She pushes her chair back and stands. "Father, you are living in the finest coffin money could buy. Peace out, Kronies."

"Brat!" Hedy yells.

Mr. Krone shoves his plate away with such force that when it glances off a floral arrangement, the carcass continues on its original trajectory—lubricated by gravy and grease— sliding across the table and coming to a stop as the new centerpiece.

Mr. Krone gets up and pulls at the bookcase door.

"Father, wait! I need twenty thousand for Milan!" Hedy blurts as she jumps up to run after him.

He slips through the secret bookcase door; it closes behind him.

In his office, he slumps into his burgundy leather Queen Anne wing-back chair.

"Your brandy, sir." Simon removes a brandy snifter from a silver tray and places it on a side table.

"Ingrates! Every one of them! I brought them up surrounded by greatness, and each figured out, in their own unique way, precisely how to rot. They are leaving me to carry the world on my shoulders. They've done nothing but bring me suffering. The Great Human Experiment is a failure."

"Will that be all, sir?"

Mr. Krone waves Simon away with a flick of his wrist.

Alone, Mr. Krone opens the center drawer of his baroque writing desk and pulls out the change purse Bill gave him.

Placing it on a sheet of paper on the desk, he turns his attention to one of his most cherished items, his Visconti Alchemy H.R.H fountain pen, set in its holder: a pair of serpents encircle the pen, each eating the others' tails. It reminds him of the A.U.'s symbol; just substitute the pen for a triangle cut gem. Wealth, Power, Control; the three sides of the triangle. In a perfectly balanced world, the A.U. sits at the center of everything.

He stares at the blank sheet of paper. After a long pause, Mr. Krone plucks the pen from its serpentine holder, slides the change purse aside, and writes:

My children respect me

With a sigh, he underlines it three times, stuffs the note in the change purse, and tosses it aside like a crumpled love letter.

Bloop.

Will takes a deep breath and runs his fingers through his hair.

"Mr. Krone was here, wasn't he?

"Yes."

"He still doesn't get it."

"What matters now is that you do." Wen plucks a change purse from the pile. "This is for you." She gestures to his chest. "May I?" She places the change purse over his heart.

"Whoa … what's happening? I'm tingling all over."

She takes her hand away, and the change purse is gone.

"Think of it as a seed. Whether it grows is up to you."

"Will Freeman, you are infinite."

TWENTY

Agent of Chaos

"Hey," Will says. "What's everyone looking at?"

The group spins around.

"Will!" Lily jumps into his arms.

"Whaaaat?" Russell does a double-take. "We just watched you get swallowed whole. Literally. How are you right there,"—he points—"and not in there?"

"Are you taller?" Lily asks. "You seem different."

"I feel different."

"Will!" Bill restrains himself. "Are you okay?"

"I'm better than okay ... I feel great."

"What happened?"

"I had a long talk in there."

"With Infinity?"

"And Wen."

"What did you talk about?" Hack asks.

"They gave me a new perspective."

"Here's a perspective," Ash gripes. "You're all clueless. He's in, then he's out. Nobody finds that suspicious?"

Hack glances at his phone. "I don't think we lost time if that's what you're inferring."

"How do you know?" Ash says. "You can't prove it."

"The security cameras would tell us," Hack says.

"Let's go," Ash says.

"Hang on. Will," Hack asks, "how long did you talk with Infinity?"

"I dunno, ten minutes?"

"That's incredible … " Hack wipes his forehead. "A CE-5 in an altered timeframe."

Lily turns to Russell, "Translation?"

"CE-5: Close Encounter"—Russell rattles off—" of the Fifth Kind: human-initiated contact with an extraterrestrial or extra-dimensional intelligence and an altered timeframe: time passed for him but not for us."

"And you got information." Hack asks. "Did you receive a download?"

"Wen called it an upgrade."

"Will, do you know what this means?" Hack paces like a professor. "This might open up an entirely new path of human evolution. This changes *everything.*"

"Stop." Ash gets in his face. "Download? Try brainwash. She's got you wrapped around her little finger with her magic tricks." Ash's charges are met with blank stares. "What? Am I the only sane one here?"

"For chrissakes, Ash," Hack counters. "Not everything is hostile."

"Did they give you access to their weapons? Huh?"

Will furrows his brow.

"Exactly, I didn't think so. She's not upgrading you … she's domesticating you. You can't see that? You're all a bunch of morons."

"Ash," Bill replies. "Don't be a hothead."

"Hothead? I'm the only one keeping us safe here. You're all brainwashed. This ain't E.T. we're dealing with. Her kind are gonna swoop in, take over, and keep you as labor or livestock … all without firing a single shot." He unholsters his pistol. "Not if I can help it."

"Ash, stand down!" Bill orders, stepping in front of his son. "You're unfit for command … not that you ever were. I'm relieving you."

"What are you gonna do, shoot a bunch of kids?" Hack asks.

"Into the break room," he gestures with his pistol. "All of you."

"Ash," Will says. "Put down the gun. You're running on fear."

"Cut the Kumbaya hippie shit."

"Your father doesn't have to control you anymore." Will continues.

"You self-righteous punk … what are you, a shrink now? You think you can analyze me?" Ash steps up to Will.

"Will, let's go," Lily says.

"Ash, lower your gun," Will says calmly.

"You think you're better than me. You think you know me." Ash pushes Will in the chest with his pistol. "You don't know me."

"You don't have to do this anymore," Will extends a hand. Ash's knuckles whiten as he tightens his grip on the gun. "Get in the god-dammed break room!"

"Your father humiliated a toddler for being afraid of spiders. He was wrong to do that. You're *afraid* …."

Ash stumbles. Furious, he sprays in Will's face. *"AFRAID?* Do I look AFRAID?"

"Ash! Don't you touch my son!" Bill yells, stepping between them.

"Your tattoo,"—Will nods to Ash's fists— "Know fear. It's not a warning … it's a confession."

"Will, stop it!" Bill admonishes.

"I'll show you afraid!" Lily yelps as Ash grabs her by the arm and presses the gun to her temple. "All of you! Get in there, *NOW!"*

"ASH! Have you lost your mind? Bill hollers. "For chrissakes, she's a *child!"*

"You think I won't, *Mr. E?"* Lily winces, her neck bent as Ash presses harder. "Get your righteous ass in there." He pushes Lily to the floor.

"Your gun …" Will points.

"What about it?"

"It's jammed."

"No, it's not."

"Yes, it is."

Ash aims it between Will's eyes. "No. It's not."

"And you're sweating."

His arm quivering, Ash pulls the trigger.

Ka-klunk.

"What the … what did you do to my gun?"

"Would any of you recognize a ruse if you saw one?" Mr. Krone slips between the gap in the hangar doors. "A.C. Activated Consciousness? Try Agent of Chaos. That's *Master Wen.*" His crooked fingers struggle to button the top button on his suit jacket. Lily stands with the group as an infirm Mr. Krone makes his way to them. "Ash, you may stand down." He lights a cigarette, blowing the first exhale in Will's face. "You've done it, my boy." He places his hand firmly on Will's shoulder; Will jerks away. "Anybody can learn to play the piano, but few will play Carnegie Hall. You, my boy … you have raw talent!

"Will, you and I share a bond. A common experience nobody else here can understand. You'll soon realize you've outgrown your friends and family … your father. It's lonely at the top. Come, take your place among giants."

"Keep your hands off my son!"

"I'm fine right where I am with my father," Will says.

"Your *father?*" Mr. Krone's chuckle is more of a mucus-filled cackle; he clears his throat. "Will, look around. Your *father* abducted you and your friends to save himself. The fact that he's your biological father is true and irrelevant."

"My father loves me."

"Love? Your father slapped you around his office. What a lovely family reunion." He points at Will with his cigarette. "Ever since Wen showed up, your life has been nothing but trouble. You think you're going crazy, don't you?"

"Don't listen to him," Bill says. "He's trying to get inside your head."

"You think I haven't spent a day in your shoes? She's blowing up your worldview so you're ripe for whatever she wants you to believe. That's how she gets you. Activated consciousness, bah! Love and light! She's conning you. You don't actually believe that stuff?"

"You're lying. I know you're lying."

"This is all by design." He waves his hands and takes a long drag off his cigarette. "Master Wen ... where is she now? Did she make you think you could talk to *birds?* She's got a good sense of humor ... talking to birds, hmph!" He coughs into his fist.

"You're a greedy, bitter old man." Will keeps his gaze on Mr. Krone.

"Perspective; that's what you got, right? Good, bad ... right, wrong; these are all human concepts ... they aren't real. We live in an entropic universe. What you or I like or dislike doesn't matter; everything descends into chaos eventually. The world doesn't need her help to fall apart. She who brings chaos brings nothing at all. He who brings order shall be king ... everything where it belongs, everything in its place."

"Every *thing* in its place hasn't gotten your children's respect."

"A father can only do so much. Greatness is that rare gem none of them could grasp. But in you, my son, I see *greatness!*"

"That's *my* son," Bill growls.

"You're an absentee father. You've lost the right to call him your son. Except for a lone dimple, he's more like me than you."

"I'm nothing like you," Will counters.

"Ah, there's where you're wrong, my son. You get me; no one else understands what we feel. You can never go home; your mother won't understand you anymore … she'll look at you just like my wife did and see a freak of nature.

"My entire family looks at me like I'm mad. If only they could go inside, they'd understand too."

"There are others," Russell says. "The Franklin Incident. The dude that got swallowed up was David Bancroft. He got an honorable discharge and spent the rest of his life in a monastery. Rumors were he could levitate and heal people."

"Know it all."

"I'm autistic. What's your excuse?"

"You're nothing but an ant at my picnic." Mr. Krone winces; with the flick of a finger, he somersaults Russell across the room. "Where were we? Oh, right, I can't open it, but you can. Now, I can finish what I started."

"You didn't *make* it open. Infinity opens when she wants."

"Tomato tomahto. What matters is you're going to open it for me." He flicks the ashes off his cigarette.

"I can't."

"I watched you do it … *twice!*"

"Infinity opens when she wants to … I can't make her." Will looks Mr. Krone in the eyes. "You want the respect of your children."

"Child, that won't work on me."

Will glances over his shoulder.

"Ash …"

Ash grabs Lily and once again puts his gun to her temple.

"Which is faster … your abilities, or that bullet? Shall we find out?"

"No!" Will yells. "Wen!"

Bang!

Ash rakes at his neck and pulls out the tranquilizer dart. He turns to see Bill with the rifle. "You baby-handed, pencil-pushing …" his eyes roll back as he collapses to the ground.

"Pity," Mr. Krone says. "He wasn't too bright anyway. All brawn, no brains." He turns to Bill. "Sleep, Bill," he says, and Bill drops to the floor like a leaf. "Anyone else care to mount a defense?"

Everyone takes a step back. Mr. Krone walks up to Infinity and presses his cigarette into her surface. Lily gasps. "Don't worry, little girl. Harder than diamonds, isn't that right, Hack?" He strokes her surface, and a charred wake follows. "It's been a very long time since I first met Infinity. You've obviously got an *in* with her. Tell her to open." He presses his hand into her; like ants fleeing a lit match, a withering blackness spreads across her surface.

"What are you doing? You're hurting her!" Will shouts.

"Wen!" He looks around frantically.

"Calling for your guardian angel?" Mr. Krone sneers. "That's sweet. Make her open …."

As Infinity's shell begins to wither, parched tendrils quickly rise and flail about.

"Stop it!" Lily screams. "You're killing her!"

"Wen!" Will shouts.

"Scream all you want," Mr. Krone says. "She's not coming." Each tendril that touches Mr. Krone crumples to the floor.

"What kind of super-sentient being doesn't know how to get out of the way?" Mr. Krone muses, producing a flask from his jacket. He pours alcohol on Infinity, flicks an ember onto her and her surface erupts in flames. Like a lobster being dropped into boiling water, an eerie scream fills the hangar while Infinity crackles.

Will shouts into the rafters. "Wen!"

"Your God has abandoned you. I would never do that."

Wen's business card flashes in Will's mind.

"*You are the Drive?*"

"NO!" With a thrust of his hand, he extinguishes Infinity's fire. A second thrust sends Mr. Krone hurtling across the hangar, landing halfway up the opposite wall.

"Will, you just accomplished what took me years to master. You're just like me. You are the son I always wanted."

"I have a father."

"It's not easy being a god, is it?"

Bang!

A dart strikes Mr. Krone in the chest.

"Noooo!" Will screams; Mr. Krone's body falls to the ground in a heap.

Will turns to see Hack holding the rifle. "Why did you shoot him?"

"Frankly, I just wanted to put that cigarette out. The sign says No Smoking."

Will runs to Mr. Krone.

"I knew you wouldn't …" Mr. Krone manages before losing consciousness.

Hack checks Mr. Krone's limp body. "He'll be sore tomorrow, but he'll survive— unfortunately. These are short-sleep doses, they'll be up soon. One moment …" Hack removes a small case from a utility vest pocket. He opens it to reveal three hypodermic needles in a bed of grey foam. "These will buy us more time … they won't remember today," he says and injects Mr. Krone and Ash.

"Look!" Lily points at Infinity. Like a potted plant finally watered, Infinity's shape and color slowly return. "She's getting better!"

"Dad, wake up," Will touches his father on the shoulder. Bill wakes with a start.

"Will! Are you okay?" Bill grabs Will and embraces him. "I'm so sorry to bring this to our family."

"Dad, it's okay. I'm okay."

"Mr. E, we need to get out of here. I put them to sleep."

"That's a good thing."

"But when they wake up, it will be a bad thing."

"Let's get the kids out of here, Hack."

"What do we do about Infinity?" Lily asks. "We can't just leave her here."

"She has to be protected. We need to move her," Hack says.

"Are you on our side now?" Will asks.

"I guess I was always on your side."

"How do we move her? Do we need a flatbed?" Russell asks.

"You don't need a flatbed." They turn and see Wen. "Will, you are the Drive. You can move her just like you moved Mr. Krone."

"Wen, that was an accident. I didn't know what I was doing …."

"You do know, Will. Attention, intention, expectation." Wen walks to the hangar wall, holds up a hand, then walks through the wall.

"Whoa! Did you see that? She walked through the freaking wall!" Russell says. "This is way better than any episode of E.E."

"Brilliant!" Hack says.

"Will, you've got to try," Lily says.

"Dad?"

"I know you can do this."

"But where do I start?"

"Son, relax."

"Yeah, relax … I got to relax." He shakes his shoulders, arms, and hands.

"Inhale, exhale," Lily adds.

"Right, inhale, exhale."

Russell taps a finger on his right temple. "Close your eyes. Be the pilot. Fly the freaking ship!"

Will closes his eyes and takes a deep breath.

"Wait." His eyes pop open. "I don't have to fly her. I move her." He approaches Infinity, closes his eyes again, and raises his hands, palms stretched outward towards Infinity. He takes a deep breath.

Bloop, bloop, bloop, bloop!

The sound fills the hangar; like a chattering octopus, colorful patterns play across Infinity's surface; eddies, rings, and speckles come and go.

From the center of Will's chest, an energetic bubble emerges and radiates outward. The bubble's colors cycle in sync with Infinity's. As the bubble expands, it hums with an electric wuh-wuh-wuh-wuh.

The bubble creates its own vortex; wind swirls in the hangar, the massive doors flap, and high windows shatter inward. Flying papers swirl, rendering visible the shape and speed of the indoor cyclone. The workbench and chair are flung to a corner; parked vehicles slide across the floor into one another.

Wuh-wuh-wuh-wuh … bloop, bloop, bloop, bloop!

Will's bubble engulfs Infinity.

Wuh-wuh-wuh-wuh … bloop, bloop, bloop, bloop!

Like a symphony nearing its crescendo, the sounds and lights pulse in harmony on both the bubble and Infinity. The bubble pops with a deafening, lyrical wuh-bloop!

The shockwave knocks Will off his feet, rips through the corrugated roof, and sends the contents of the hangar flying. Will feels a hand grab his ankle and pull him across the cement floor. Will feels the weight of his father on him, shielding him from flying debris.

When the wind stops, the only sound left is the creaking cry of the corrugated ceiling as it dangles from the hangar's opened wound.

"Is everyone alright?" Bill calls out.

"Where's Infinity?" Russell asks Will.

"She's off the grid."

"Off the grid?" Bill asks.

"Yeah, Dad, *off the grid.*"

◦ ◦ ◦

With a twist and a pull, Bill gets the ring over his knuckle and off. He chucks it in the predawn field.

"Everybody into the green car," Bill orders.

"Mr. Freeman,"—Russell chases after him—"that's my brother's …"

"This car's not bugged." Bill opens the driver's side door and hops in.

Hack emerges from the hangar with two cases and a backpack. "Pop the trunk. We'll need this."

"What are they?" Lily asks.

"Air soldiers," Bill says. "Drones … military grade."

"Please, don't insult them." Hack clarifies, "They're Roids: Recon and Tactical Assault. The military wishes they had these."

"What about Deb?" Bill asks.

"No worries. I have her little sister right here," he shows off his backpack. "She might be little, but she packs the biggest wallop." With a mischievous grin, he adds, "Mr. E, did you really think I would let that monster have this kind of power?"

"It'll be a tight squeeze in this little car, but I'm so glad you're on our team."

"Will, remind me … is it the Meredith or Plymouth exit?"

"Meredith?" Lily asks. "That's way up north."

"We're going off the grid." Bill answers.

"I'll remember once we get close." Will's voice softens. "Dad?"

"Yeah?"

"What about Mom?"

∘ ∘ ∘

Beep, beep, beep.

Fingers clumsily search for the snooze button on the phone. *Sleep. Just one more minute of lovely, lovely sleep.* With a pillow-muffled, "Ughh," Rod rolls onto his back. "Now's when the fish are bitin'." With a long stretch, he forces himself awake, opens his sleeping bag, and sits up on the cot, resting his feet where he lay his socks in the night. The yellow light of dawn filters into the cabin; specks of dust hang in a sunbeam like far-off stars drifting about in the heavens. He grabs his t-shirt off the floor and slips it on.

"Coffee, coffee …" Sifting through his duffel bag, he pulls out a bag of coffee. He gets up, and with one hand holding the bag and the other scratching his camouflage boxers, he shuffles to the front door.

"Good morning, sunshine!" He throws open the door. His jaw and coffee bag both drop at the sight. Blocking his view of the pond is a sizable boulder resembling a giant three-sided football covered in barnacles and seaweed.

"What the f…."

www.ingramcontent.com/pod-product-compliance
Lightning Source LLC
Chambersburg PA
CBHW021313190726
48288CB00003B/830